brixton
bwoy

ROCKY CARR

brixton *bwoy*

A NOVEL

FOURTH ESTATE · *London*

*For my parents, and
for Jeremy and Judy*

First published in 1998 by
Fourth Estate Limited
6 Salem Road
London W2 4BU

1 3 5 7 9 10 8 6 4 2

A catalogue record for this book is available from the
British Library.

ISBN 1 85702 738 8

The publisher and the author would like to thank
Patricia Salkey for permission to reproduce
'A Song for England' by her late husband, Andrew Salkey.

Typeset by MATS, Southend-on-Sea, Essex
Printed by Clays Ltd, St Ives plc

A Song for England

An a so de rain a-fall
An a so de snow a-rain

An a so de fog a-fall
An a so de sun a-fail

An a so de seasons mix
An a so de bag-o-tricks

But a so me understan
De misery o de Englishman.

Andrew Salkey

Contents

Ackee and Saltfish

'Have we got everyting?' Pops called.

'Yeah,' came back the chorus.

'Come on den, we go catch some fish.'

It was dark, pitch dark. There was no electricity in this part of Jamaica. It was rough country. From the hill near the house they could see the lights of distant towns, and Pupatee would sometimes stand there and admire the red and blue and white dots glowing in the darkness. But tonight they had their torches; Pops turned them upside down and soaked the wicks and lit them. The dogs drew back and spread themselves around the house, as if they understood they were in charge until the masters returned.

Pupatee and his older brother Carl, the last of the twelve brothers and sisters left at home, loved night fishing.

'Why we go night fishing, Pops?' Pupatee asked.

'Because de fishes sleep at night,' Pops said. His playful slap around the ear nearly took off Pupatee's head. He was a big man, Pops, sometimes he didn't know his own strength.

That afternoon, Pupatee and Carl had run home from

school as fast as they could through the fields and forest, and over the streams and hills, ignoring the coconuts and cucumbers and guava and sugar-cane they could have picked along the way. They did not even stop in the mad woman's orchards to steal her sweet limes or number eleven mangoes. When they got home, Mama gave them a good dinner of ackee and saltfish, with pumpkin and rice and avocado pears, and after they had eaten all they could, they took the herd down the river to drink. The animals sucked eagerly at the clear flowing water, which was so clean that the family would drink it straight from their cupped hands, and swim in it too on a scorching day.

While Pupatee and Carl had been away, Mama and Pops had cut some bamboo stems in the forest, and they were now working them into fish pots and spear sticks. The cattle were safely back in their pasture, so the boys joined in. They cut more lengths of bamboo at their joints, which formed a kind of cup. They pierced holes in the cups, poured paraffin through the holes into the lengths of bamboo below and rammed bits of crocos-bag material in after it.

When they were ready, Pops lit the boys' torches and they walked in silence back down to the river. The night air was cool. Mama walked straight into the water with a fish basket which she held, gently moving, under the river banks. Suddenly she snatched it out and when the water had escaped there was a whole pile of fish flapping about at the bottom of the basket. Mama was tall and God-fearing, with a smile that never failed to make Pupatee quiver with happiness.

The fish were passed up to the boys, who gutted and cleaned them and put them in a bag container. Then they ran after Mama and Pops to see what they had caught next.

If fish were sleeping, Pops, and sometimes Carl, speared them or chopped them with cutlasses. While Pupatee watched, Pops and Carl turned over rocks in the water and almost every time found a long fat juicy eel lying there. After putting down the rock carefully so as not to wake the eel, Pops aimed for the head and chopped fast and clean.

Mama said, 'Inu ush little.' They all froze.

'Ah wha?' Pops whispered.

'A whole eap ah sand fish sleeping next to each other. Me ah go try scrape some up in de basket ca dem so slippery you lucky to catch one otherwise.'

Mama bent down and moved in with the basket, catching four big sand fish, which was quite a rare piece of luck. As they all celebrated, Pupatee stumbled on a group of big red crayfish, their snappers sharp and ready to clip predatory fingers. He called his brother and when he was near enough Pupatee plunged both hands into the shallow water, grabbed two large crayfish, and flung them out of the water on to the land. Carl also dived in and caught one, and laughed because it was the biggest and fattest of the lot.

The night deepened, but none of them cared. Pops was chopping more fishes, while Mama and Carl were catching them with their bare hands under the bank. Pupatee was frightened of putting his hands into that gloomy water below the bank where they might touch something like a water snake or an angry eel, but when Mama and Carl and Pops put their hands in they usually came up with plenty of fish, or at worst grass and muddy rubbish.

Making their way down the river, they came to a large rock in the water with two entrances into the space beneath it. 'Bet a large eel live under here,' Pops said. Carl covered one entrance with his sharp pointed

3

cutlass while Pops took care of the other. They checked with each other and thrust deep into the entrances at the same time; both smiled as they felt their weapons go into something soft. They put them down and picked up the rock, and there lay two large eels, each speared right through, floundering helplessly.

After three hours Pops said they should call it a night. They had collected so many fish that they had to leave some there in shallow water to stay fresh until they could return to carry a second load. Then they staggered home. They had plenty of different lovely fish. Although it was still the middle of the night, Mama started straight away seasoning the fish and salting the eels, putting on a big pot to boil up soup as well as a pan to deep-fry small fishes which they would eat whole, bones, eyes and all.

By sun-up, people from nearby were starting to come past to see if any fish were for sale. When Mama showed them the rare sand fish and the crayfish and eels, the buyers started bidding the highest prices.

Word soon got around, and before long young women and girls started arriving to help Mama sort out and cook all the fish. Pops was drinking rum with his friends, and Carl and Pupatee and some of the other boys went to collect coconuts full of milk for them to chase it with. (Sometimes Pops would make 'Manhood punch' with rum, eggs, condensed milk and oats – he said they would never have any trouble with the ladies while they drank it.) The morning ended with a huge feast of fried and steamed fish, fish soup with bread and crackers, all kinds of vegetables – pumpkin, breadfruit, plantain, gungo beans, callaloo and corn – and plenty of sugar-cane for those who weren't keen on fish. The night's successes were shared, and no one went away unsatisfied.

*

4

The restless lowing of cattle woke Pupatee and his brother from their midday rest. They picked up their soap and towels and led the herd to the river, where they washed and splashed about to cool off while the cows drank thirstily. After a while the boys realised how tired they were – they hadn't slept a wink all night – so they got out and began to drive the cows quickly away from the river. One of Pops's strictest rules was not to rush the herd, especially if any of them were carrying calves. But being tired and eager to get home, Carl pushed Pops's cows too hard, and one panicked and fell into a big ditch.

They went for Pops and when he realised what had happened, he started fuming because it was his best cow, which was in calf. 'Ah sorry fe de two ah you backside later,' he shouted. They dragged the injured cow nearer home to keep an eye on it.

Back at the house, he turned and stared at the boys. 'Carl, a you de one rush de cow mek she brek her back in de hole?'

'No, ah no me!' Carl protested.

'Pupatee, ah must be you den!'

'Ah no me, Pops,' Pupatee cried.

'Was it Carl?' he demanded, and Pupatee was so confused and frightened of Pops that he forgot that he should have said no, and he nodded his head and said, 'Yes.'

'Me know it was you!' Pops shouted at Carl. 'Me ah go give you backside a good beating fe dat. You wait and see, Mister Carl.' Carl looked at his younger brother, and Pupatee wanted the world to open up and swallow him for what he had said. All that day, Carl didn't talk to Pupatee once or laugh or play with him. He wouldn't even let Pupatee walk next to him. That night after dinner Pops caught Carl and gave him a

5

bad beating, and afterwards Carl cursed both Pops and Pupatee.

The next day was Sunday. Hoping that he would be left behind on his own, Pupatee told Mama he was sick and couldn't go to church. To his horror, Mama told Carl to stay behind too, to look after him. While she was at church, and Pops at his sugar-cane meeting, Gamper, one of their older sons, who lived with his women near by, between Gurver Ground and Cross Hill, turned up. He said he was going swimming with some friends, and invited Carl and Pupatee to go along. All the men and boys ended up down at the river by Mathew's Deep Hole, named after a man who had drowned there. When the water was calm no one would believe it could run so deep. Soon Gamper and his friends James and Puttie were diving and swimming happily at one end, while Edward and Esau, the youngest, were playing in the shallows.

'Come on Pupatee, follow me,' said Carl. Pupatee laughed and followed him, excited that his brother was talking to him again. 'Follow me, follow me,' Carl kept saying as he swam backwards into the river. Pupatee followed, only to find himself in the deep hole with the current pulling him down, and Carl backing away.

A panic suddenly gripped Pupatee, and he began to splash about, trying to shout for help. He could see Gamper and his friends not far from where he was, but every time he opened his mouth to shout, water poured in and muffled his cry. He looked around for Carl, but by now he realised that his brother, his best friend, had left him to die.

Years later, Pupatee could still remember that moment. The world seemed to slow down almost to a stillness. Suddenly he stopped panicking and looked around calmly, seeing and hearing everything –

Gamper and his friends swimming, Edward and Esau playing, the wonderful greenery surrounding the still water, the laughter and voices, even the birds singing. 'Lord have mercy,' Pupatee said to himself, and prepared to go. But as he was on his last breath, ready to meet his end, he heard a voice call, 'Wait! Weh Pupatee deh?'

Making one last struggle to stay afloat, Pupatee lifted his head and saw Gamper and his friends stop what they were doing and look all around with frightened expressions on their faces. Then one of them shouted, 'See him deh ah drown over deh!' Another voice said, 'See how you save man ya,' and a figure made a large dive. When he came up he had Pupatee in his arms and was taking the boy to the shore. The others helped him and pumped water out of Pupatee's lungs.

Gamper said, 'You all right, Pupatee? How long you did ah drown for?' As he tried to answer, water ran out of his mouth. 'Wha you go in ah de deep hole for, bwoy? You mad? You no know seh ah dere Mathew drown? Ah Mathew Deep Hole, dat.'

He smacked both his younger brothers as he cried, 'What would me tell Mama and Pops?' Then he sent them home and told them not to mention a thing. Pupatee never did say a word, and after that the disagreement between him and Carl was ended. Carl had forgiven him, and Pupatee never thought to blame his brother. They were back to their normal selves, happily fetching and bringing back Pops's herd from the river, cutting the grass in the sunlight, fishing and swimming.

Pupatee and Carl didn't like to miss out on the big tasty dinners the grown-ups ate, but they had to be at

7

the table at the correct mealtimes. Pupatee was unlucky and often late, so he and his brother soon became very good at 'wild bush cooking'. They would make their own fishing rods and lines, and cook up tasty fish dinners outdoors using whatever vegetables and spices they could help themselves to. The weather was always hot and while their stew simmered they would sit in the shade listening to the birds squabbling in the branches above them.

Every Saturday without fail, Mama used to boil up a big pot of soup. All Jamaicans love soup; they believe it keeps them strong and wards off common illnesses. Mama was a fine cook and Pupatee loved her pea soup best of all. He used to watch it keenly, waiting in the delicious coconut-scented steam for the moment when it would at last be ready. Once he ate so much of it that he had no room left to breathe.

The rooster on the roof woke the household every morning.

'Time fe go milk de cows dem,' Pops would shout, his big body blocking the doorway. 'We coming, Pops,' the boys would call back to him as they rushed to wash and dress.

When the milking was over, Pops would send Carl and Pupatee out with the donkeys to cut grass for the cows, and woe betide them if they tried to cut corners and just cut the grass from the shade, rather than out in the open, where the sun had prepared it for the cows' bellies.

By the time all this was done, and the boys had eaten their breakfast of fried saltfish, fried and roast dumpling, fresh hot chocolate and hard dough bread, and had run across the fields and streams, and up the hills, and down through the trees, they were often late for school. The first time this had happened, when

Pupatee was only six years old, he had got a terrible shock.

The teacher sent Pupatee straight to see Mr Sweeney the headmaster. He found Carl already there, standing with his hand stretched out in front of all the older boys and girls. Pupatee went over and stood beside him. Carl whispered, 'Take dem all pon one hand, Pupatee.'

The next thing he saw was a thick leather belt coming down three times on his brother's hand. Carl didn't make a noise, but after the third hit he put his hand between his legs to cool it. Then the headmaster turned to Pupatee. It was his turn. The girls in the class were all whimpering and saying, 'Oh no, not a little boy like dat.'

'Hush up!' The headmaster's voice echoed around the classroom until everything was still and silent again. 'Stretch out you hand,' he demanded.

It took the terrified Pupatee a moment to understand what he had said. Fright stopped him lifting up either his left or his right hand. When he did finally manage to get some movement from his hands, both came up together. The class burst out laughing, and Mr Sweeney grew even more furious.

'Put one hand down, bwoy!' he shouted. Pupatee tried to obey, but he was so nervous that both hands went down at once. There was another burst of laughter, which the headmaster cut short with a fierce look at the boys and girls behind him.

Mr Sweeney's eyes then returned to Pupatee. He quickly lifted his left hand and the headmaster looked at him as if to say he was going to make these ones especially sweet. Slowly, he raised the thick leather belt. At the top he paused for a moment – and then he brought it down with such force that it was no wonder that when the belt reached the spot where it was supposed to connect with Pupatee's hand, the hand was no longer there. The hand had returned to Pupatee's side, and the belt swung through empty air until it landed with a slap on the headmaster's own leg.

Now Mr Sweeney was really mad. 'Ah six you ah go get instead ah tree if you no hold out you hand,' he yelled. Pupatee looked at him for signs of mercy, but he just shouted again, 'Bwoy, hold out you hand.'

Pupatee held it out, and closed his eyes, and the next moment he felt the fire spread across his palm. When the pain hit the tender part on the inside, he started jumping as if he was doing a rain dance.

It was a while before Pupatee was ready to put up his hand again. It had become shy and he couldn't keep it still. Then that 'Bwoy, stretch out you hand' echoed through his ears again, and he put up his right hand this time. Mr Sweeney looked at him as if to dare him to move it again, and Pupatee closed his eyes as he took the lash. This second one was worse than the first and when the pain hit him Pupatee was jumping up and down like a stallion being mounted for the first time. Then he found himself on his knees, with his hand under his arm, as if expecting a gushing waterfall from his armpit to put out the fire that was now running through his hand and up the nerves into his body.

'Only one more to go,' the headmaster said, bending down to look at Pupatee. Through his tears, Pupatee could swear that for a moment he saw a look of sympathy on the man's face, but then that hard look and stare returned and his voice boomed out.

'Get up and hold out your hand, bwoy!'

Pupatee sprang to his feet, because he sensed the headmaster was about to start with his 'six instead of three' voice again. But now he didn't know which hand to offer as they were both stinging like pepper in the eye.

'Come on, bwoy. Me got a class to teach!'

He stretched out his left hand and a mighty whack came down on it. It was the last, and Pupatee fled out of the school screaming, found a tap and ran his hands under the cold water.

The first person who came to his rescue was Carl. 'Me tell you fe tek dem pon one hand instead ah can't use two hands.'

'Me right hand no too sore, man,' Pupatee managed to say.

Carl laughed and said, 'Come, before dem beat we again.' Then he led his little brother back inside.

After that, every week it was the same, and before long if they were late, Pupatee would persuade Carl to stay away from school for the whole day, running free through the countryside instead. And when they did go to school, although Carl was a good student, Pupatee learned almost nothing. He could just about spell his name, but not any more than that. He didn't even know his alphabet, and it was all he could do to count to ten. He would just sit in school, and wait for the afternoon to end.

After school, life began. A whole group of them would set off to pick sweet limes and number eleven mangoes. The best grew on land owned by a woman they thought was mad. She would lie in wait for them and when they were in the middle of picking the juiciest fruit, high up in the trees like the doctor birds, she would jump out and surprise them, shouting, 'You tief inu me catch you all tiefing me mangoes. Police, police!' and they would run off as fast as Pops's animals ran down to the river in June.

*

11

One morning, after cutting the grass and eating breakfast, Pupatee was late for school as usual. There was no sense hurrying now – Pupatee would get a beating whatever – so he dawdled, and Pops saw him 'You na go ah school today, Pupatee?' he called. 'What wrong with you?'

'Me pencil no sharp, Pops.'

'Come, me sharpen it fe you, come.'

Pupatee followed him into the house and he took out his big, long razor. He was proud of this razor, and he took great care of it, cleaning and polishing it after every use. He opened it out and the blade shone as silver as the moon. He calmly sharpened the pencil and replaced the blade in the handle, winking at Pupatee and smiling.

'Den de teacher na go beat you, man, de way you so late.'

From outside, Carl shouted, 'Pupatee, de later we are ah de hotter de licks, you know. So you better come on, we half late already, ah!'

'Me gone, Pops,' Pupatee said.

'All right, massah, me see you.'

Pupatee joined up with Carl, but he was walking slowly. 'You no have fe hurry now, ca wha me no go anywhere near dat school deh today, fe me get no tree licks ah no dis or dat from headmaster, prefecs or Mama or Pops. Me know a nice place we can go over de mad woman place, go pick number eleven mangoes and bully mangoes and blackie mangoes and custard apples, mmm.'

Pupatee was all excited and ready to venture anywhere with his brother. Before long they found a family of Aba palm trees, whose nuts turned from green to bright yellow when ripe and tasted like miniature coconuts. Pupatee was up those trees quicker than a monkey, selecting the ripest and best, eating as he found them. 'Look, ah number eleven mango tree. Dem big and ripe. No true, Pupatee?' Carl shouted. Pupatee looked over from the tree where he was and it was a beautiful sight, all those mangoes, some red, some green, some light yellow, hanging from every limb of the tree. He came down the Aba palm faster than a snake and was soon gorging on the sweetest and juiciest mangoes.

Later they came across jackfruit, and they found sweet limes and pawpaws, and suddenly Carl said, 'Look, bully mangoes,' and Pupatee couldn't believe what he saw – mangoes as big as his head. Pupatee had never seen them so big, and he could only manage one while Carl had two. This adventure went on all day, and the brothers were so full of fruit when they returned home that evening, they could scarcely eat their supper.

At school the next day, Pupatee used his newly sharpened pencil so much that he blunted it. He decided to sharpen it himself, and stole into the house the following morning to borrow Pops's razor. Pops was so skilful with his razor that Pupatee had never understood how delicate that sharp blade was, and a big chunk snapped off in his hands. Horrified, Pupatee quickly put the blade back and crept out of the room even more quietly than he had come in. He ran all the way to school, and that day he was so downcast that the teacher asked him if he was ill. It was Friday, and Pupatee knew there would be a beating that weekend. All the next day, nothing happened, but on Sunday, after milking the cows, Pops announced he was going for a shave.

A few moments later, it happened. 'Who use me razor and broke it up?' Pupatee's heart started beating fast – he knew he was in danger now. When Pops came out, he and Carl took off and luckily escaped, with Pops cursing after them. He was so mad it didn't matter whose fault it was.

'Oh no,' Carl said, when they were far enough away for safety. 'If him catch me, me ah go pretend me ah dead, ca him must kill we wid beating when him catch we.'

'How you go pretend, Carl?' Pupatee asked.

'Just play dead wid froth coming out your mouth, and when the licks reach go'on like you can't feel it, dat is how.'

They had to come home for dinner. It was fresh fried fish and eels with roast plantain and turned roast breadfruit, Pupatee's favourite, but although he was starving, he couldn't eat through worry. And anyway, they were only half-way through eating when Pops returned. He came straight for Pupatee, shouting, 'Why did you broke me razor, bwoy?'

'Me never meant it, Pops, do no beat me, Pops,' Pupatee cried. 'You ah beg, please no, do no.'

'Ah going to bust you rass today,' Pops cried, and he pulled out his belt and began to beat Pupatee.

Pupatee waited for the first three or four licks, and then put Carl's plan into action. He went limp and began to collect spit in his mouth. After another three lashes, Pops realised something was wrong. He stopped.

'Pupatee! Pupatee! Pupatee!' he cried. 'Kay, come see, him ah dead, Kay!'

'Me ah come,' his mother answered.

'Pupatee!' Pops was calling again. By now Pupatee had a mouthful of frothy saliva, and he let it bubble through his lips. Pops stared down at him and began to shake him.

'Lord, Putoo,' Mama cried. 'You ah kill me wash-belly pickney!'

'Me never did start ah beat him hard yet, Kay,' his father protested while Mama picked him up and took him to his bed, where she rubbed ointment into his sores and aches.

That day, Pupatee was left to sleep, and for several days he was given tip-top treatment while he pretended to recover slowly. Even Pops came in to tell him he was sorry and he would never beat him again as long as he lived.

For weeks after that, Pops kept his word. Everywhere Pupatee went, he heard the neighbours whispering that he was the boy who had almost been beaten to death by his father. And Pops didn't raise a hand against him. But then, when the incident had almost been forgotten, Pupatee irritated Pops and he swung out at him and caught him on his arm. It was hardly a lashing, certainly not a beating, but handiwork was there again for everyone to see.

'From me born me never see ah boy pickney soft like gal pickney so,' Pops protested to Mama. 'One little slap and his arm swell up so. Dat is it, I will never put me hand pon dat boy ever again.'

'Lord God have mercy, man, it looks like you broke him arm.'

Pupatee wanted to laugh, but he managed not to. From that day, his father never again laid a hand on him. Pops had a heart as big as this world, though nobody could see it for it was hidden away deep in his chest. Often in the years to come, Pupatee would remember how Pops had reacted to the pain he had caused: horrified by what he had done to the son he loved.

This was how life was. One year, when Pupatee was

eight years old, they got news that their son Joe would be coming home for Christmas. Carl and Pupatee had a whole heap of brothers and sisters in England and America, some of whom they had not seen since they were babies, and some they had never seen. Joe was the oldest of them all, the first son, and he had not been home for many years.

The closer it got to Christmas the hotter it became. Most of the mangoes and other fruits were out of season until the next year, so they turned their minds to other food. There were many tasty birds to catch, like the pea dove, the ground dove and the white-winged and barby doves. These birds were easy to pluck and clean and Mama was always pleased when the boys brought them home. She cooked them over a raw fire, either pierced with a stick and rubbed with salt and seasoning, or fried with garlic, onions and peppers.

At the fine news that Joe was coming, Pops killed a couple of chickens. A few days later, he killed a couple of ducks and a big fat pig. Finally, they slaughtered two goats and invited all the neighbours round, saying Christmas had come early that year.

The day before Christmas Eve there was a big clean-up, and all the neighbours went home to get ready for their own family feasts. Joe arrived that night. Carl and Pupatee were very excited to see this brother who was like a stranger, and Mama and Pops were full of happiness at the return of their eldest son. The house seemed almost fit to burst with anticipation. When Joe walked through the door he didn't let them down. He was not a big man, but he was dressed in slick English clothes, and when he spoke his voice was high and his English perfect. Pupatee had to concentrate to understand him when he talked.

Joe had gone to England many years before. He lived

in London with his wife and children, and had a job as a van driver for British Rail. He seemed very old to Pupatee – he was, in fact, old enough to be his father. Carl and Pupatee were very proud to have such a big brother. They stayed up as late as they could listening to the talk until Mama noticed the time and sent them up to bed.

The next morning, the rooster woke the house with a triple cock-a-doodle-doo alarm. Mama and Pops were dressed straight away and headed through the door to get their daily chores done early. Carl and Pupatee were washed and dressed early too. They helped Mama light the log fire and then went to help Pops milk the cows. When they brought the milk back to the kitchen, Mama asked Pops if he was going to kill another goat to celebrate Joe's arrival.

'Wha? A little goat?' Pops replied. 'Wha you ah talk seh woman, we son come home from faran country and you ah tell me fe kill just one little goat! Oh no, we ah go kill one fat bull fe him. When him ah go back we can kill one little goat, yes, but me would be too shame fe kill just a goat fe him arrival!'

Mama was laughing, and Carl and Pupatee looked at each other in amazement. A fat bull! That meant pure beef for Christmas!

'Carl, Pupatee.'

'Yes, Pops.'

'Go get de youngest, fattest bull and bring him down to de slaughter post.'

'Yes, Pops.'

Just then, Joe walked into the kitchen and wished everybody a good morning.

'Ho, you get up already,' said Pops. 'Good, you can help me kill one fat bull we killing fe you welcoming home,' said Pops.

'That sounds like my kind of talk,' said Joe.

Mama was still smiling with delight as Carl and Pupatee went for the fatted bull while Joe and Pops got rope and a big sharp knife, and when the boys returned with a young beefy bull, Pops and Joe tied it to the slaughtering post.

Before they could begin, Mama called everyone for breakfast. They all sat around the big table in the kitchen and ate their bellies full of fresh hot chocolate, saltfish fritters, fried dumplings, salt-fried pork with callaloo greens and two big half-ripe roasted breadfruits as extras. While Mama started cleaning up in the kitchen, Pops and Joe took a bottle of white rum and two coconuts with milk inside for a chaser, and went and sat in the sun near the bull at the slaughtering post.

Carl and Pupatee were left in the kitchen to help clean up and after a while an argument started. It was over something trivial, a fishing weight, but soon they were readying for a fight. First Carl hit Pupatee, and just as Pupatee drew back his fist to hit him back, Joe walked into the kitchen. He needed a file to sharpen the knife that was to be used to kill the fatted bull.

'What!' cried Joe, taking off his belt and giving Pupatee a few whacks. 'How dare you hit your elder brother. Don't you ever do that again.'

Tears poured down Pupatee's face. It wasn't the pain, but the shock of being hit by his brother Joe, who he so idolised.

'Wha wrong with you bwoy, wha you ah cry for?' Pops asked.

'I caught him throwing punches at his elder brother and gave him a slight belting,' Joe said.

Pops laughed and Pupatee turned round to see a smile on Joe's face, which only put him in an even hotter temper.

18

'Pupatee, wha you ah cry like a girl for?' said Mama when she saw him coming towards her, sniffing away.

'Nothing.'

'Come, me comb you head fe you, son.'

Pupatee went to her. Mama's warmth was comforting, and he felt better after she had oiled and combed his hair. 'You look nice now, Pupatee,' she said. He smiled.

Outside, Pops and Joe were tying up the bull so that it would not be a danger during its slaughtering. The post was an old stump of a tree, still attached to its roots. After a while the bull was trussed to the post by its horns, and it looked fierce no longer, but frightened. It mooed and tried to pull itself free, but its struggles were useless.

Carl appeared with a large container to catch the blood for the dogs. Pops offered Joe the big slaughtering knife to do the killing, but Joe refused. Pops smiled. 'Faran country changed you a lot, son, you used to love doing de killing years ago.'

'Can Pupatee do it, Pops?' Pupatee said. They all turned to see him watching them from the veranda.

'You still a pickney, bwoy, dis a man work.' Pops laughed, then he looked at him and said, 'Pupatee, you no remember de time when you kill Massah Tom little pig?'

He did remember. An animal had been raiding one of Pops's far-off vegetable fields every night and Pops had grown so weary that he had offered his sons a pile of money if they caught it and killed it. So one day, Gamper and Carl packed a tent, food, knives, cutlasses and machetes and walked to this far-off field. They set up their tent and slept at the spot where they expected the intruder would try to get into the field. That night,

19

it showed up just as they hoped. It turned out to be a very large sow, bigger even than them. The boys were frightened, but they wanted the money even more than they were afraid of the harm that sow might do them. So Gamper charged at the sow and dived on it with a long sharp knife. The sow put up a strong fight, trying to escape from Gamper and Carl. Even after its throat had been cut, it stumbled several yards before it finally fell down and lay still.

Mama and Pops had made much of Gamper and Carl, giving them their money and praising them to the skies. So when, several months later, Pupatee came across a piglet, he pulled out his knife and killed it. But no one had told him to kill this piglet, and it wasn't even trespassing, so instead of getting a hero's welcome, Pupatee got only a good beating.

'Pupatee! Pupatee?'

'Yeah, Pops?'

'You deaf?'

He shook himself out of his trance. Joe and Carl tied a rope to the back legs of the bull and Pops took the knife and pulled it across the underside of the bull's neck, cutting right through and almost taking its head off. The blood gushed out and fell into the waiting container. The bull made one last deathly moo, kicking and quivering all over, and as the blood poured from its throat, the dogs began to gather.

'Pupatee, you and Carl go bath, den go tell de people you big bredda Joe deh home from England, and one big whole dinner get together ah ran fe him. And me, and you Mama, ah invite everyone. Also tell dem on sale is fresh beef. Tell dem me kill de best bull and plenty good food is here.'

'OK, Pops.'

'And son, go tell de whole ah you cousins and dem

20

friends fe come help Mama,' said Mama. 'And hurry, Pupatee.'

That night, when darkness fell, they had a great feast of beef from the slaughtered bull. They built a big fire and roasted nuts and all kinds of other goodies, like breadfruits, sweet potatoes, fish, birds, yam and sweet corn. There was rice and peas, boiled pumpkin and plates of fried green bananas. Everybody joined in the fun of lighting fire crackers and big loud bangers and rockets which flew up and exploded with a wonderful brightness in the pitch dark. And all the time people were playing music and dancing and singing. Pupatee's disagreement with Carl, and even his beating from Joe, was soon forgotten, and it was the biggest and best Christmas ever.

A few days later it was time for Joe to go back to England. The whole family were sitting together, Pupatee between Mama and Pops. Then Mama said, 'Joe, me ah beg you. One last favour for Mama, do son.'

'What is it?' asked Joe.

'By de time Pupatee and Carl done looking after dem fadda's cows, dem always late fe school and Pupatee no even badda go sometimes. Lord have mercy pon me, Joe, me wash-belly pickney no even know two letter out de ABCDEFGH, so me would ah glad if him could ah come ah England wid you, to go school, where him would ah learn fe spell and write him name.'

'Oh no, Mama,' Pupatee stuttered. He was happy at home with Mama and Pops and Carl. But to his horror, Joe agreed.

'I suppose he could wash my car on Sundays,' he said. 'You can send him over in a few weeks.'

And that was that. There was nothing Pupatee could do. Mama had made up her mind and he was going to England. After all, Joe was there and so was another brother and several of his sisters. Pupatee would be looked after fine.

When the day finally came for Pupatee to leave for England, his father was not his normal self. Pops barely looked at him or said goodbye. He didn't want his youngest son to go, but he hadn't been able to persuade his wife. She was a determined woman. Mama, Carl and Pupatee left Pops behind and set out for town, where they stayed overnight, and the next day they made their way to the airport.

At last the moment came when they all stood by the escalator that would take Pupatee to the plane and away from everything familiar.

'Bye Mama, bye Carl,' he said quietly, turning to start up the escalator.

'Wait!' Mama cried. 'You not going to kiss Mama before you go to England?'

Pupatee ran back and threw himself at his mother, hugging and kissing her. Then she gently sent him on his way. As he was carried along on the escalator, tears dripped on to his shoes. It was the first escalator he had ever seen.

2

Fish and Chips in the Snow

The world was white and when Pupatee bent down and picked up some of it, it was cold, like the ice he knew from drinks called skyjuice or snowballs back in Jamaica. He shivered and stuffed his hands deep in his pockets and walked out on to the slippery pavement of Selborne Road, Camberwell. The snow was on cars, on rooftops, on the branches of trees. It seemed to have taken the place of leaves. He wondered why there were no leaves on the trees.

Pupatee watched a group of children across the street playing with the snow, scooping it up and throwing it at each other. A skinny white boy with yellow hair slipped some down the back of a girl and made her scream. A moment later the children were all ducking and sliding and laughing, having the time of their lives. In the distance Pupatee heard a train rattle by.

He walked on alone, marvelling at the sights of this new world. The people were various colours, black and white and yellow. The streets were filled with cars and lined with huge buildings. It was all so tall and enclosed. Pupatee stepped gingerly along, his feet unsure beneath him in his tightly laced new shoes. Cars slid down the roads, where the white snow had turned to a grey slush. People in thick coats walked hurriedly along. He passed the Odeon picture house and a huge walled building that was King's College Hospital. A little further along, white people in long coats were queuing up at a window, buying food wrapped in newspaper. The smell of frying oil made him realise he was hungry, so he turned the corner and headed back in the direction of his brother's house.

As he approached Selborne Road, he saw the kids had stopped playing with the snow. Some of the faces had changed, but he recognised the skinny boy with blond hair and blue eyes. He was dressed in blue jeans and black boots, and he had a blue and red anorak with a fur-lined hood hanging down behind. A white scarf was wrapped twice round his neck with its ends dangling below his waist. Pupatee felt very under-dressed. The boy's shoulders were hunched and he was hugging himself against the cold. As Pupatee walked by, the boy looked at him and shouted out, 'Ha, I think I seen you somewhere before, mate. Was it Africa?' At this, all the other children burst out laughing. Pupatee stood there puzzled. He barely understood the words and he certainly didn't get the joke. He was so cold his blood seemed to be turning to ice in his veins.

'What's your name, mate?' the skinny boy asked, his voice softening as if he felt bad for making fun of him. Pupatee understood this question. 'Pupatee,' he replied.

This set the whole gang laughing again. When they had calmed down, the only black boy among them said, 'That's an old man's name. How old are you, Pupatee? About seventy-five?' They were all in stitches now, while Pupatee stood there, frozen with misery and shock. 'Pupatee,' the black boy said. 'Pupatee, bet you are the good-looking one in your family.'

Pupatee understood enough of this to feel the shame begin to burn inside him. While they carried on laughing, he turned down his face. When he found the door, he ran inside and washed his face so Miss Utel, Joe's wife, would not know Pupatee had been crying.

Miss Utel was in the kitchen. She was short and had shiny dark skin, and when she flashed her smile her single gold tooth would twinkle. Her black hair was bunched on top of her head, streaked with a single block of grey. She wore a thick white woolly pullover and a black knee-length skirt with a big button at the waist. She always wore blue slippers in the house. Pupatee liked her.

'You hungry, Pupatee?' she called out.

'Yes,' he answered, when he had finished washing. Strange smells were wafting up from the stove where Miss Utel was cooking. They certainly didn't smell like ackee and saltfish and Mama's hot chocolate, and when Miss Utel put the plate down in front of him Pupatee couldn't identify what was on it. The only thing Pupatee recognised was the egg. The rest were like strangers to him: sausages, fish fingers and baked beans. But he was famished, and he loved eating. He would get used to bland English food, but he would never stop thinking about fried fish and plantain and allspice, and mangoes that tasted like sunshine.

Brother Joe had gone to work early. Joe and Miss Utel had five children, Johnny, Terry, Tracy, Lena and a baby girl still in arms named Jasmine. The older kids had gone off to school.

'Me ah go school too?' Pupatee asked Miss Utel. He felt comfortable alone with her and less strange, but he was anxious not to be left out.

'No, Pupatee. You don't start school until we sort it out with the head teacher,' she explained. 'And you must get accustomed to the way they speak in England, because they don't rate the patois. Pupatee, are you listening to me?'

'Yes, Miss Utel, but me no understand one word yet.'

'Oh dear me.' She laughed. 'Try to talk like everyone else in England. You understand that?'

'Me understand little ah it no much,' he said, confused by this new language.

While Pupatee ate his food, Miss Utel tried to simplify it for him. 'Look, Pupatee, patois is broken English,' she said.

'How dem broke it, Miss Utel?'

She laughed again. 'Cho me we mek de kids show you later.' This time, Pupatee laughed too, as he realised she could talk Jamaican. 'You understand dat, no?'

Pupatee nodded, happier.

'You ah fe learn fe chat English,' she said.

'But me no want talk English, man!'

'If you brother Joe hear you seh dat him beat you, you see, man?'

'How Pupatee talk English?' The words almost flew out of his mouth. He had already felt Joe's beating in Jamaica.

'Well, if you no hear wha someone seh, instead you say "wha", you say "pardon", or "beg your pardon", not "wha you seh".'

'Oh, me see wha you mean.'

'And when you see wha someone mean or you hear wha dem seh, you seh, "Pupatee understand" or "fair enough".'

'Fear enough,' Pupatee managed to say.

'Yes, that's good. I'd better go back to English talk now or when your brother comes home I will say to him, "See you dinner yah!" and he will kill me in this house tonight.'

*

26

There was much to learn in England. Pupatee had already discovered the miracle of lights and light switches. In Jamaica, he had seldom seen electric lights except from afar, twinkling in the dark night. But now he was staying in a house full of lights which he could turn on and off. Then there was the television. He had played at school with a Viewmaster, a plastic box that displayed slides, but television was something else. When it came on that first afternoon he stared in amazement. He tried speaking to the people inside, but they didn't seem to hear him. Unworried, he sat down to watch. It seemed only a minute later that his nephews and nieces piled home from school, laughing and shouting. Pupatee stood up and vacated his chair so Johnny and Terry, who were older than him, could claim their places in front of the television.

'Have you all said good evening to your Uncle Pupatee?' Miss Utel scolded them. 'Good evening,' they chorused, and everyone laughed. Pupatee joined in and none of them could stop. For the first time Pupatee almost felt at home. Miss Utel was kind and his nephews and nieces were friendly enough. He hadn't chosen to leave the sun of Jamaica for this new, cold, white land. But he was ready to make the most of it.

For the first few days, Pupatee did not see much of his brother. Joe worked as a driver for British Rail and when he came home after work, still in his grey uniform and cap, he would unloosen his tie and put his feet up, and Miss Utel would bring him his dinner. By the time he was finished and ready for a few beers and some television, the children were going to bed.

Pupatee slept in a room with Johnny and Terry. On his second or third night, he wet his bed. He was nine years old, and he felt ashamed, so he washed his pyjamas himself and hung them out on the line to dry, as he would have done in Jamaica. That night, he had undressed before he realised his pyjamas were still outside. He ran naked downstairs and out into the garden to fetch them. They were still wet and cold. On his way back, the other children saw him. Their laughter carried through to the sitting-room.

'What is it?' Joe's voice boomed through the house. The next thing Pupatee knew he was in the hall, glowering at him.

'Boy, what are you doing, put some clothes on!' he shouted, taking off his belt as he did so. Pupatee stood there, quaking with cold and fear. Joe raised his belt and then brought it down on his brother's bare flesh, giving him lash after lash. The children had vanished but Miss Utel came out and cried and pleaded with Joe to stop. Pupatee ran upstairs, dragging the unwearable pyjamas behind him. As he lay shivering in bed, he vowed he would not make any more mistakes and prayed that Joe would not beat him again. It was a prayer Pupatee would repeat over and over until he eventually lost faith in receiving any response. For in that house, Joe's word and belt were law.

In those first few weeks, before Pupatee went to school, he set about exploring this strange new world. Selborne Road was as different from the farm in Jamaica as snow from hot sun. There was a constant rumble of traffic along the hard streets, and the only birds he heard were the pigeons cooing on the rooftops. Terraced houses, some with four or five bedrooms and three floors, were packed in side by side, full of people. There were far more buildings than trees.

Camberwell in those days had a very mixed population. Pupatee had seen different sorts of people in Jamaica, but nothing to compare to this. There were

West Indians, Africans, Chinese, Indians and Irish, as well as ordinary white English people, all living close together. Although Pupatee was aware that he was different from many of them, and jokes were made about the colour of his skin, he never thought of it as a problem. Kids of all sorts played together. If there were divisions, they were not between races, but age groups. The kids were in league against the world of adults, and they stuck together.

Before long, Pupatee began getting to know the local kids. The skinny white boy who had called out to him that first day was Jimmy, a coalman's son and the leader of all the kids in the neighbourhood. The black boy who had teased him was Lass, Jimmy's right-hand man. As Lass carried on making fun of him, Pupatee became used to being the object of jokes, and eventually he even began to join in.

Sometimes Pupatee would accompany the other boys down to Ruskin Park, where he was relieved to see all the big trees, though dismayed at how bare they were. He looked in vain for mangoes or oranges, but these English trees had nothing on them worth eating.

Pupatee had never seen so many shops. There was a sweet shop and a newsagent that sold papers and magazines and birthday cards, and a big Turkish café near the traffic lights. There was a hardware store crammed to the ceiling with wallpaper, paraffin, brooms, planks of wood and tins of shiny nails. Next door there was a cake shop and Pupatee would always stop to stare at the tarts and pies and pastries topped with fruit icing. There was a shop that sold carpets and a shop that sold musical instruments; toy shops and bicycle shops, a bookie, and a store that was packed with car parts. There was a greengrocer, but it didn't have any pawpaw or breadfruit. Next to the Odeon there was a pet shop that had mice and goldfish and kittens in the window, a butcher, a flower stall, and a fish-and-chip shop that filled the street with the smells of frying food. Pupatee couldn't believe his eyes when he saw all these shops. In Jamaica he had only ever known two.

Pupatee also met some of his family. He had four sisters in England. Kathleen and Annette lived in Birmingham, so he only met them occasionally, but Pearl and Ivy were in London, only a bus ride away, and whenever Pupatee could pluck up his courage he would ask Joe if he could go and visit them.

Pearl lived in Brixton, seven stops away on the 45 or 35 bus, while Ivy was another nine stops on from Pearl. Pearl and Ivy were hard-working housewives, both of them gentle and kind, mothers of three and four children respectively. Pupatee felt comforted and at ease when he was with his sisters, especially Pearl who lived in Kellett Road with her husband, Mr H, and her three children, Roland, Richie and Selena. Roland was a year older than him and he and Pupatee soon became fast friends. In time, he took the place of Carl, whose companionship Pupatee sorely missed. For the next few years Brixton, with sister Pearl's love and Roland's friendship, would be an occasional haven from life in Camberwell with Joe.

By this time, Joe was beating Pupatee regularly. Pupatee had quickly learned not to put even the smallest foot out of place in Joe's house – but something would always go wrong. One day, Pupatee was playing with his nephews Johnny and Terry in the back yard, and he forgot himself and swore. Johnny ran inside like a bullet. 'Mum, Mum, Pupatee said "blood claat".'

'What?' Miss Utel said. 'Pupatee, come here! What

30

kind of bad words are you using in front of the children?'

'Ah no dat me seh, Miss Utel.'

'Never mind, man, tell it to your brother when he comes in.'

His worrying started there, for Joe was due home any minute, and it was not long before he arrived like the Devil himself.

I'm glad you've come in time to talk to your brother,' Miss Utel said. 'Swearing in front of the children.' She must have known it would mean a beating for him. Swearing was strictly forbidden.

'What!' cried Joe, and before Pupatee could move he was slapping him with his hand. Then he took off his belt and lashed him with it repeatedly. When it was done Pupatee crept to bed, frightened and lonely. He lay there miserably, thinking how far he was from home – but it was no use hoping Mama or Pops could help him now. He would write a few clumsy words to them whenever Joe told him to, and from time to time they would write back. But they were a long way off, and he couldn't tell them how he really felt. They were in Jamaica and out of sight, and he was here in England with no prospect of going home. So as time passed and Pupatee learned to be self-reliant, his parents slowly faded further and further from his thoughts.

Even when Joe was out, Pupatee was never entirely happy, for Joe's behaviour hung over his life like a shadow. After a while, whenever six o'clock drew near, Pupatee would start to feel sick and tired, for that was the time when Joe came home and he was likely to get another beating. The worst thing was when he had done something early in the day, and Miss Utel would tell him that Joe would hear about it later. Sometimes he did not understand what it was he had done wrong, and it seemed even she had given up on him. But on the occasions when he was aware of his crime, the anticipation and fear would ruin his whole day just the same. And when Joe came home and heard what Pupatee had done Pupatee would see the rage spreading over his brother who would bite his lip at the prospect of the punishment he would exact. He would order the boy upstairs, and tell him to take off all his clothes except his underpants and wait for him there.

One black day, after a beating with Joe's belt, Pupatee foolishly told the children it hadn't hurt. He was overheard by Joe and Miss Utel. Miss Utel only laughed, but Joe started biting his lip and giving Pupatee that crazed look. The next time Pupatee was judged to have done something wrong, Joe really beat him, using flex wire from an old electric heater. The wire was thick, and plaited together. That beating really hurt.

Sometimes Miss Utel would feel sorry for Pupatee. Joe would beat her too. In the time Pupatee lived in the same house as Miss Utel, blows from Joe broke her nose and her arm. Joe was easier on his own children, but even they were frightened to death of him. But he reserved his best – or his worst – for Pupatee. Everything Pupatee did was wrong. Unlike Pops, who had stopped beating Pupatee when he thought he had hurt him, Joe had no pity. 'Get up the stairs!' he would shout, and his voice echoed in Pupatee's mind like Big Ben tolling the time.

Pupatee tried everything, from begging Joe for mercy to letting the flex hit him across the face and putting his hands to his eyes and screaming, 'Lord, bredda, me eye, woo ho, please bredda, do!' But somehow it seemed that this only got Joe more excited and angry. Once, Pupatee tried the trick that had worked so well with Pops and pretended that Joe had beaten him unconscious. But it didn't dampen Joe's enthusiasm for the task, and he just carried on with the beating until the licks made Pupatee revive again. 'Bredda, no lick me no more, do!' Pupatee cried, and then Joe only lashed him harder for having played dead and tried to decoy his way out of the punishment.

By now, Pupatee had started primary school. The school was a collection of tall flats, buildings and houses surrounded by red-brick walls and a strong, tall wire fence. There were three sets of gates leading into the playground, and the big wooden doors were reinforced with iron to make them doubly secure. All the windows were covered with iron grilles secured with padlocks.

It was good forgetting about the house, about Joe, but school wasn't much easier than home. Pupatee's English was now much improved, but he could still barely read or write and the teachers didn't have time to give him the help he needed.

At first he did not understand many of the customs and games. The girls teased him and the boys picked him last in games of football. But one day, Pupatee was given a chance to prove himself at school. He was playing marbles in the playground with Flego, a boy he had become friendly with, when the school bully, Dave, and his gang came over and began to push Flego around about some argument that had happened before Pupatee's arrival. When one of Dave's shoves pushed Flego over, Pupatee rushed over to his friend and picked him up.

'Hey bwoy, go away!' Pupatee screamed at the bully.

'What, you want some too?'

Dave came forward, but Pupatee's childhood fishing

and swimming and climbing trees in Jamaica had strengthened him, and the beatings Joe administered had made him resilient, and unafraid of someone as small as Dave. Dave hit out at Pupatee, but then Pupatee threw a punch into his opponent's belly which felled him. He lay gasping on the ground while Pupatee stood over him.

That earned Pupatee a reputation, and whenever a fight started up in the playground, he was seldom far away. He usually won. He had found a way to impress the other boys and make a name for himself. It did not occur to him that he had learned this talent from Joe, from the very beatings he himself so hated and feared.

Not all Pupatee's time with boys his own age was spent fighting, though. Out of school, he hung around with the local gang led by Jimmy and Lass. Jimmy was the life and soul of the streets around Selborne Road. He had the blond hair and blue eyes that the girls liked, and a winning combination of mischievousness and vulnerability. He was always the first to come up with something fun to do, the first with a joke.

His father drove a coal truck and Jimmy would often help him, coming home after a session shovelling coal almost as black as Pupatee. 'Yeah, man,' Jimmy would say while putting his arm on Pupatee's shoulders. 'Dis is my brother, who just come from Jamaica, man.' And when Jimmy had cleaned himself up, he would pull the same stunt. 'As you can see, ladies and gents,' he would declare, 'I'm a bit paler than my brother today, because I'm a bit ill.' Although most of the boys were white like Jimmy, black kids like Lass and Pupatee were treated as equals. In Jimmy's gang, colour counted for nothing.

Gang life revolved around bicycles, and Pupatee was the only one without his own. After school and at weekends and in the holidays, Jimmy and Lass and

the others would get on their bikes and pedal off to
Ruskin Park or some steep hill they wanted to try out,
and Pupatee would be left behind. He soon longed for a
bike even more than he longed for his home in
Jamaica. Life with Mama and Pops and Carl was a
distant dream now, but a bicycle was real.

One half-term, when Jimmy and the gang had gone
off elsewhere, Pupatee was walking down the street
where an African family whose kids went to the same
primary school as him were packing their belongings
into a big removal van. He stopped to talk to them and
the boys told him they were going back to Africa.
Pupatee pretended to listen, but what really interested
him was the brand new, shiny push-bike in the van. He
said goodbye and walked off, but he kept looking
behind him, and as soon as the coast was clear he ran
back, jumped into the van and took the bike.

All that day, Pupatee taught himself to ride. He fell
off a hundred times and kept smashing the bike, and
by the end of the day it looked twenty years old. The
wheels were buckled and the paint was scratched, but
Pupatee wasn't bothered; he couldn't take it home
anyway. He parked it somewhere it could easily be
seen, hoping that someone else would take it. Then he
went home where he found Miss Utel cooking. They
were chatting happily in the kitchen when there was a
knock at the front door. Pupatee went to answer it and
his eyes almost popped out of his head with shock. It
was the father of the African family.

'What did you do with my son's bike?' the man said.
'Somebody saw you steal it so there's no point denying
it.'

Miss Utel had come to the door. 'Can I help you
please,' she said stiffly.

'I want my son's bike,' the man repeated. 'Somebody

saw this boy steal it and somebody else saw him ride it around.'

'We don't know anything about your bike,' Miss Utel said. 'You will have to come back later when his brother is home.'

'That bike cost a lot of money, madam.'

'Come back after six, to see his brother.'

With that, the man reluctantly left, vowing to return at six. Miss Utel grabbed Pupatee. 'Look,' she said, 'you know your brother will half kill you if these people come back and tell him all this, so if you know where the bike is, go give it back quick. You have time.'

Pupatee dashed out to find the bike. But when he reached the spot where he had left it, the bike was gone. He had walked sadly home, certain of a beating now.

Joe walked in not long after Pupatee. Miss Utel softened him up by giving him his dinner and stroking his head and smiling and joking with him. When she thought the time was right, she told him about the bike. Joe threw his tray with all the food aside and dived straight at Pupatee, knocking him to the ground and then pulling him up and punching and kicking him. In the middle of all this, the African man turned up again.

While Joe went to the door, Pupatee fled down into the cellar. He had taken enough and he felt he couldn't go on with these beatings. Down in the cellar he knew there was some rat poison. He emptied half the box of poison into a cup and added water and then drank it down as quickly as he could. He waited for death more happily than he ever waited for one of Joe's beatings. But that poison could not have been strong enough, for death didn't come. It was not his time. And when he crawled to bed that night Pupatee was black and blue from Joe's beating.

*

36

Sometimes Pupatee's friends took pity on him, and went to places on foot so he could come too; sometimes he managed to borrow a bike and explore further afield with them. Jimmy and the others liked having Pupatee around. He was growing bigger and stronger every day, and if anyone crossed the boys, Pupatee would fight their cause. With every skirmish he won he liked fighting more and more. He watched *The Saint, Dangerman* and *The Man from Uncle* on television, and practised hitting and kicking the way the men did in those shows.

One time he and the gang all went down to an adventure playground in Peckham Park. The main attraction was a sliding handle on a rope slung between a platform and the ground. Pupatee had just climbed up to the top of the platform when a white boy slid the handle fast back up the rope and it hit Pupatee smack in the face. He was so surprised he nearly fell off the platform, but he managed to hang on with one hand while rubbing his face with the other. He looked down and saw the boy in stitches.

'Wha you done dat for?' Pupatee screamed.

'You should have caught it,' the boy laughed back.

That was it. Pupatee couldn't slide down fast enough and when he hit the ground he confronted the boy. Before they could come to blows, one of the keepers broke them up and threw them both out. They left, followed by the other boys, who wanted to see what would happen. They walked out on to the grass away from the keepers, and it was agreed that Pupatee and the white boy would fight alone. Pupatee was fuming and threw the first blow. The boy came in close and swung at him but Pupatee ducked and then flung himself around his opponent's middle. They wrestled to the ground, trying to get the best of each other.

The other boy soon began to tire, but Pupatee was still strong. With one hand he held the boy down and with the other he fired a blow to his face. He heard the other's breath escape and saw his eyes and nose suddenly gush red. He was just about to throw a final punch when Jimmy stepped in. Jimmy was never one for violence – he relied on a quick tongue and sharp humour to win his battles – and he dragged Pupatee off, telling him he did not need to win the same fight twice.

Pupatee allowed himself to be pulled away, but he felt better for that fight, as he always did when he won. Without his realising it, he had learned from Joe that there was pleasure to be had from violence. He enjoyed the power his growing physical strength gave him, and being victorious over others in the playground made the beatings from Joe easier to tolerate. But he also envied Jimmy's way with words, and listened to his friend.

One evening, not long after the fight outside Peckham Park, Pupatee went round to Jimmy's house to see if he would come and play.

Jimmy's mother said hello to him, and then she called up the stairs, 'Jimmy? Pupatee is here. Get out of that bath, you've been in there long enough.'

Jimmy didn't answer.

'He's been in there for ages,' Jimmy's mum said. 'Jimmy!' she bawled out again. 'Jimmy!'

She shrugged her shoulders and turned and went up the stairs to get him. Pupatee listened to her footsteps on the landing as she called out his friend's name again. There was still no answer. He heard her knock and then the creak of the opening door.

'Oh, my God! Mick! Oh, my God!' The words were

screamed through the whole house. Jimmy's dad and brother came out of the living-room. 'What is it?' they called.

'Oh, my God, get an ambulance! Jimmy's drowned!'

Jimmy's dad and brother ran up the stairs. Pupatee still stood by the open front door listening to the despairing talk. He heard Jimmy's father say that it must have been the boiler; the pilot light must have gone out and the gas had leaked, putting Jimmy to sleep and then he had drowned. By this time, half the street had come out of their houses to see what the screaming was all about.

'He's not dead, is he?' someone asked.

Pupatee stood there in shock, fighting back the tears. No, Pupatee told himself, Jimmy couldn't die just like that.

'Someone call an ambulance,' screamed another voice.

'It's already on its way.'

And so everyone waited on their doorsteps and on the pavement, wondering when the ambulance would come. But it took half an hour to get there, and when it did finally arrive Pupatee was even more frightened, as he saw them take his friend out on a stretcher. They had put tubes in his mouth to feed oxygen to his lungs, but he looked pale and lifeless.

There was a whole crowd now, screaming and crying, as well as Jimmy's family and friends. The ambulance drove away up the Selborne Road to King's College Hospital, but it did not bring Jimmy back. A little later, Pupatee went over to the hospital and saw Jimmy's brother coming out.

'Is he all right?' Pupatee asked.

'He's dead,' his brother managed to get out. This brother was normally a big strong young man, but now he seemed to have shrunk with distress and sorrow. Pupatee stood outside the hospital for a while, and then made his way back to the house. Pupatee thought Jimmy would come running out to play any minute. He couldn't accept that his best friend would no longer laugh with him again.

Jimmy was buried the following Friday in the pouring rain at the cemetery in Peckham. The church was filled with mourners of all ages and colours. There were many boys from Jimmy's school, and girls and boys from other local comprehensives. They were all gathered around Jimmy's coffin. The priest gave his sermon. He said that Jimmy had been robbed of his life which had only just begun, but that he could only be going to a better place from this world of devastation in which we must try to continue our lives. And then everyone sang 'Rock of Ages, Pledge for Me' and they went outside into the graveyard, towards the hole which had been dug, ready for Jimmy. Pupatee saw Jimmy's mum and dad. Both were dressed in black. His mum, who had always been such a cheerful, beautiful woman, had turned old and withered. The priest said some prayers and then sprinkled earth on top of Jimmy's little coffin. Jimmy's dad looked down into the hole as if to say: Don't go, son, come back to your dad, and he seemed to want to jump into the grave. It took his friends to hold him back.

You couldn't see the tears for the rain. There were red eyes and running noses. Pupatee thought of the funeral he had gone to in Jamaica with all the laughter and music, the feast of food and drinking, the singing and the wailing and the praying. And then he, too, noticed that he was crying and he took out his handkerchief to wipe the rain and the tears from his face.

The priest left and the mourners slipped away, taking Jimmy's mum and dad with them. It was the saddest thing Pupatee had ever seen. A few weeks later Jimmy's family moved away from Camberwell. Pupatee never saw them again.

3

Brother Joe

As time passed, Pupatee settled into his life in South
London. Even after a couple of years he still missed his
brother Carl, and the freedom and colour of his outdoor
life in Jamaica, but as he made new friends and
learned new ways, the acute homesickness of the early
days receded. His English had improved, school was
bearable now he was gaining respect from his peers for
his toughness in the playground, and although he still
received regular beatings from Joe, he had learned to
mind them less.

One morning, Pupatee woke up late for school. He
leaped out of bed and ran down the stairs, pulling on
his clothes. 'Why didn't anybody wake me?' he called.
Miss Utel and all the children were standing in the
hall, dressed in their Sunday best. Half the furniture
was missing from the house. Through the open door
Pupatee could see a big blue removals van.

'We've finished putting everything in the van,
Mummy,' Terry was saying. 'Are they ready to go now?'

'Hold on a minute, Terry,' Miss Utel said, turning to
Pupatee. 'Pupatee, I am sorry I can't take you with
me. You are not my child, you will have to stay with
your brother.' She fished into her purse and pulled

out a few shillings. 'Take this, Pupatee. Goodbye.'

He took the money and stared at her, and beyond to Terry and Johnny and the rest all waiting to leave. Miss Utel turned as if to go, but suddenly she stopped and he saw a look of worry and concern on her face. 'Pupatee,' she said, 'when you grow up, don't kill Joe for what he put you through. He is your brother.' Then she walked out the door and Pupatee watched the van drive away.

For the rest of that day, all Pupatee could do was wait for his brother to come home. When Joe opened the front door, he immediately realised what had happened. A string of insults flew from his mouth, and Pupatee prepared himself for the worst, but for the first time he saw something else beneath his brother's anger. Joe looked lost.

'Fucking prostitute,' he said. He shook his head as if trying to banish all thoughts of Miss Utel and his children from his mind. Then he walked into the kitchen, which was bare apart from a few old plates and cups and saucepans – though Miss Utel had been good enough to leave some food.

Pupatee was curious at his brother's unusual behaviour and followed him quietly. He watched Joe standing there with a vexed look on his face, trying to work out what he was going to do. Joe sighed heavily. 'Pupatee,' he shouted loudly, unaware that the boy was right behind him.

'Here, bredda.'

'Oh, you're there. Now listen carefully. I am going to teach you how to cook, because if I don't work we won't be able to eat and if I have to come home and cook as well, then one night I'll drop dead.'

'Yes, bredda.'

Joe turned immediately to the counter, saying no

more about Miss Utel, and took out a packet of white rice.

'Put this in a container and pick it,' he said. 'Take out all the black bits and the dirt and stones.' While Pupatee did this, Joe took some cabbage and a knife and told him to watch what he did. 'You cut the cabbage in half like this and cut up one half fine. Then you put three pots with water on the stove.' He put the cabbage in one pot. 'Don't put too much water with the cabbage,' he said, 'otherwise it will boil out to sogginess. It should be steam cooked, you see?'

Then he showed Pupatee how to chop up saltfish, which he put in the second pot. 'You boil it to get the salt out,' he said. By now, Pupatee had finished picking the rice, and he washed it and tipped it into the third pot.

Then Joe put a Dutch oven on the stove and poured oil on to the bottom. 'Cut this onion up,' he said, 'and chop this garlic fine.' When Pupatee had done this, the garlic and onions began to fry and a delicious smell rose from the pan. 'Now you add butter and salt and a small onion to the rice,' Joe said, 'and leave it on a low fire to bubble away.'

By this time, the saltfish was soft and the salt had boiled away into the water. Joe took it out and pulled the flesh off the bone. Then he added it to the frying garlic and onions, and seasoned the dish with chilli peppers, curry powder, turmeric, thyme and salt. Soon the beautiful smell of Jamaican cooking was filling the kitchen, and Pupatee's mind wandered happily. His reverie didn't last long.

'When the fish is ready, you can add it to the cabbage and let it all simmer up together. Now you got all that?'

'Yes, bredda.'

'Tell me how you start then.'

Pupatee's mind raced, searching for the beginning, but all he could think about was how cross Joe suddenly looked and how he didn't want him to get any crosser.

'Wash the rice,' he said.

Slap! Joe's hand smacked the side of Pupatee's head.

'What about picking it?' he boomed out.

'Yes, and pick it,' Pupatee said, recalling what he had done. 'Put the rice in to cook, adding salt and onion.'

Slap! 'What about butter?'

'Yes, butter, bredda. Then put the saltfish on to boil.'

'Good. Then what?'

Pupatee gathered his thoughts, not wanting to get it wrong, but he took too long to answer and another slap startled him.

'Fry the onions and garlic after cutting them up and placing them in the Dutch pan with seasoning like curry and salt.' He thought he was doing pretty well.

'And?'

His mind was blank.

'And? And? And?' Slap! 'Put the fish in with the cabbage!'

'Yes, fish with cabbage.'

For all the slaps, Pupatee had to admit the smell was now delicious.

While the food was cooking, Joe told him to get a bottle of Guinness from the bar.

'And now go and take the eyes out of three eggs.'

Pupatee felt completely lost. How did you take the eyes out of eggs? Out of chickens, yes. But eggs?

'Why are you standing there holding the eggs like you are a statue, bwoy?' Joe shouted, putting his head round the kitchen door. 'Give them to me.' He cracked the eggs in a bowl and pointed to the small white dots

45

in the egg. 'Those are the eyes,' he said. 'They are the beginning of what would have been the hatched chicken.'

Pupatee took out the eyes.

'Now add vanilla and whip them up good,' Joe said. When Pupatee had done this, Joe added half a tin of Nestlé's milk and nutmeg and told him to whip the mixture up again. Finally, on Joe's instruction, Pupatee poured the Guinness into the bowl and whipped it all up one more time.

'That's punch,' Joe said. 'Get a pen and paper and write it all down. You can cook this for dinner on Mondays.' Pupatee found a pen and wrote some notes as best he could. He could still barely write, but the slaps had written the recipes into his memory. And by the end of the following weekend, Joe had taught him how to cook a different dinner for every day of the week.

Sunday was always the culinary climax. For breakfast, Pupatee would cook fried eggs, bacon, tomatoes and fried dumplings or plantain with porridge of either oats or corn meal. He would already have cleaned and seasoned some chicken, lamb or beef the previous day and soaked peas in water with thyme and garlic. Around noon he would put the peas on to cook and start browning the meat in the Dutch oven. When it was brown all over, he would add onion, pepper, garlic and water and leave it to simmer on a low fire until a tasty gravy formed. Dinner would finally be served with rice, sometimes washed down with a drink made from carrot juice, Nestlé's milk, nutmeg, eggs and vanilla, mixed with ice.

And so Pupatee soon fell into the routine of keeping house for Joe. When he came home from school he would clean all the rooms and then start cooking the evening meal. On Saturdays he would go down to

Brixton to get the ingredients for the week's meals, as well as toiletries and other essentials. The West Indian shops there sold many of the foods Pupatee had eaten in Jamaica, and he came to love cooking as it took him back to his parents' house and the smells of the meals his mother made. Although the place was quiet now with just the two of them in it, Pupatee preferred this tasty food to Miss Utel's meals, and he enjoyed being master of the kitchen. Even Joe seemed to appreciate the food, though he would never say so.

Joe and Pupatee were never able to finish all of the Sunday dinner, so on Monday Pupatee would simply add a bit of fish or corn meal to the leftovers, with perhaps some green bananas and a few boiled dumplings rolled out of plain flour and water, with a touch of salt. On Tuesday he would cook a tin of mackerel, with onions, garlic and seasoning, accompanied by white rice and pineapple punch. Wednesday would be ackee and saltfish and West Indian vegetables – yams, green bananas, plantain, dumplings and pumpkin. On Thursdays, he generally made corned beef and cabbage with white rice and Mackeson punch, and on Friday it was strictly fried fish with hard dough bread. On returning from the shops on Saturday, Pupatee would put on a big pot for chicken, beef or mutton soup, first boiling the meat, adding salt, thyme, fresh peppers, garlic and onion, and later, when the meat was tender, also putting in yams, green bananas, coco, dasheen, dumplings, pumpkin and a touch of black pepper and butter. He would let it all simmer away on the stove for hours, until its mouth-watering smell permeated the whole house.

Joe had turned Pupatee into a fine cook. But each evening when he came home from work, he would not touch any of his dinner until he had seen his young brother eat some first. It wasn't until years later that Pupatee understood why. Joe's cruelty to the boy had made him paranoid, and he was convinced Pupatee would try to poison him. Pupatee didn't realise this at the time, but he did get his own back in a small way. Whenever Joe told him to taste what was on his plate, he would cut off the juiciest, leanest bit of meat to eat in front of him, winning a small skirmish even as he was losing the war.

It was not long after Miss Utel had taken the six kids and walked out on Joe that Pupatee started going to evening classes organised by his school. There were classes in cookery, art, woodwork, metalwork and dancing, but it was the boxing classes which attracted Pupatee. He had already had plenty of practice fighting outside the ring, and he took to the sport like a duck to water. After a couple of lessons, his teacher said he showed promise. He gave Pupatee a form for Joe to sign, to show that he had permission to keep up the training, and Pupatee hurried home with it, flushed with excitement. He was certain in his heart that if he worked hard he could be like his hero Muhammad Ali. How proud Mama would be of her wash-belly son when he became the next world champ.

Eventually Pupatee plucked up the courage to show the form to Joe. 'If you sign this,' he told him, 'the teachers say they will train me into a boxer.' Joe's only response was to bite his lip as he always did when he was about to inflict a lashing, and order Pupatee upstairs to strip off. He was barely undressed before Joe stormed in and first a right and then a left fist slammed into his body, followed by a head-butt which landed him on the floor in a daze. As Joe kicked Pupatee with his heavy boots, he yelled, 'You couldn't

48

punch your way out of a wet paper bag.' Then he pushed the bruised and aching boy downstairs to scrub the kitchen floor.

Pupatee's excitement about becoming a boxer had disappeared. His only ambition now was to grow big and strong enough so that one day Joe couldn't hurt him any more. With each wring of the floor cloth, Pupatee's determination to make something of himself receded. So long as he could survive, he didn't mind what became of him.

Not long after this, Joe told Pupatee he had found a job for him, working each morning for Bill the milkman. Early every morning, Bill would knock on the door and Pupatee would run out to help him.

Bill was a big fat white man who sweated as he ran from his float to the doorways to deliver the milk. 'One red top and one gold top at number ten, Pupatee,' he would shout as he ran in one direction, expecting Pupatee to run in the other. 'Two gold and one silver to number fifty-six.' Bill covered a large area, from Camberwell Green up past King's College Hospital. He was fit for a fat man, and never paused for breath until the milk round was finished. By then, Pupatee was already tired and even less inclined to pay attention at school. And although at the end of every week Bill gave Pupatee his ten bobs' wages, Pupatee had to give this straight to Joe. He wasn't allowed to keep a single penny for himself.

One morning, when Pupatee went to a particular house to deliver the usual milk, he found a note saying the family had gone away on holiday and had left Bill the money they owed. Wrapped inside the folded paper was a crisp one-pound note and a few coins. 'Three red tops at number twelve and one gold and a silver at number thirteen,' Bill called. For a moment Pupatee hesitated, and then he slipped the money into his pocket.

From then on, Pupatee made sure he got a bit of pocket-money every week. Sometimes Bill would even be expecting people to leave money and he would send Pupatee to look for cash inside a bottle or under a mat.

'What you got?' he would ask.

'Nothing,' Pupatee would say as he artfully pocketed the money.

Bill would mutter and curse under his breath. Then he would say, 'OK, put three red tops at number twelve and one gold and a silver at number thirteen.'

Sometimes, if Pupatee smashed a few bottles by accident, or Bill felt his assistant wasn't working hard enough, the milkman would lose his temper. And he had some horrible habits, such as easing his backside off the driving seat to let out an almighty fart, which would boom like an explosion while he commented, 'Cor, that 'urt!' But Bill was usually smiling and happy by the time they delivered the last bottle and were on their way home.

Nevertheless, Pupatee carried on stealing Bill's money, and would sometimes lift a bottle of orange or a pack of sausages from the cart before leaving.

One morning, after Joe had given Pupatee a really bad beating, Pupatee was in such pain that he could barely walk. 'Run, can't you,' Bill shouted at him. 'You're slower than my crippled granny.'

Pupatee couldn't go any faster. His arms and legs and back were all black and blue with bruises. When Bill and Pupatee got back to the float, the milkman stopped to look at him properly for the first time, and noticed his swollen eyes and lips.

'Oh, my God,' he cried. 'Who did that to you?' He had a look of total disgust on his face and he started muttering about calling a policeman. Pupatee was surprised at Bill's concern. He had suspected that what Joe did to him was unearthly, but seeing the horror and disgust on Bill's face he realised for the first time quite how wrong it was. Bill's reaction reminded Pupatee of what his mother and father showed to him back in Jamaica whenever he was hurt or ill. It was affection, or even a sort of love, perhaps. But he still couldn't tell Bill that it was Joe who had beaten him.

'Some skinheads,' he said finally.

'Mother of Jesus,' Bill said. 'What did they hit you with? How many of them were there? Where did it happen?'

'Er, round de, round de green.'

'Christ,' Bill said. 'What did your brother do? He must have blown his top, innit?'

All this suddenly made Pupatee feel very confused. Bill seemed to care for him more than his own brother. Back in Jamaica, there had been beatings, but not like the ones Joe delivered. If Carl and Pupatee had been expecting a beating they would stay out after dark until Pops forgot about it. Sometimes, in the years before Pops stopped beating him altogether, Pops would even call out, 'Pupatee, if you worry dat we ah go beat you fe de wrong, you do no badda hide. Come, we na go beat you again. We will feget it, come in, Pupatee.'

For a while Bill treated Pupatee with real gentleness, but Pupatee was too foolish to welcome this affection and he continued to steal from Bill, pocketing the money left in milk bottles and raiding Bill's ice-box. Eventually, the milkman could not fail to realise what his assistant was doing.

At first, he tried questioning the boy and when Pupatee denied everything, he would curse him. When

51

that didn't work, he tried to clout Pupatee a couple of times, but Pupatee lashed back at him, jabbing at his face and huge belly, and he backed away. In the end, Bill decided he had had enough and one morning he gave Pupatee three weeks' wages and told him he was sacked.

Joe was furious when he found out, but fortunately Bill had been kind enough not to mention his suspicions and simply told him he thought Pupatee was old enough to get a better-paid job. Joe might have been a violent and intolerant man who fell far short of being any sort of father figure, but he was always scrupulously honest, and any hint of thievery would have brought the full weight of his anger down on Pupatee.

Even when stealing from Bill, Pupatee never saved much money – certainly not enough to buy a bicycle, which was what he wanted more than anything. But shortly after Pupatee lost his job on the milk round, Joe bought himself a car and stopped using his own bicycle to go to work.

One day during the holidays, Pupatee worked up enough courage to borrow the bike in Joe's absence and soon he was sailing round the block to meet up with the other boys. At first they laughed, because Pupatee's bike was old-fashioned and heavy, but they soon changed their tune. It might not be any good for doing wheelies, but it was fast and powerfully built, and Pupatee won many of the races.

Flushed with his first day's success, Pupatee dared to borrow Joe's bike for a second day of hanging around with the other boys, racing up and down the road. In the lead in one race, Pupatee turned to see the others hard on his tail and he started to pedal furiously, picking up so much speed that he took the corner too wide. The next thing he knew he was crashing into a new car belonging to one of the other bikers' dads. Pupatee was OK and even Joe's bike showed no signs of damage, but one side of the car was badly scratched and dented.

The car's owner hurried out, took one look at it and said, 'Someone will have to pay for this.' He turned to Pupatee. 'Where do you live, boy? Come on, we'll go and sort this out with your family.'

'No, Dad,' Pupatee's friend protested. 'His brother will kill him.'

'Shut up, boy. Who is going to pay for the car, so I can go to work and feed you?'

Pupatee had no option but to take him round to Selborne Road. When they found the house empty, the man fumed even more. 'All right,' he said. 'Tell your brother I'll call back another time to discuss the damage to my car. You hear, boy?'

Of course, Pupatee had no intention of telling Joe anything. But when his brother came home Pupatee could barely hide his nervousness. He kept peering through the curtains to see if his friend's dad was on his way round. He considered telling Joe the truth, and getting the beating over and done with, before dismissing this again. He tried to work out where he would be able to hide. Every time he heard footsteps on the pavement outside his heart would thump. It grew later and later and he was beginning to think he might escape that evening when there was a knock at the door.

'Who is that?' said Joe.

Reluctantly, Pupatee went to answer it. His fears were realised: his friend's dad stood on the steps.

'Your brother in, boy?' he asked, in a voice that

53

suggested it was the end of the world for Pupatee.

Joe came to the door looking confused. 'Didn't he tell you what he did to my car?' asked the man.

'No.'

So he told Joe how Pupatee had scraped up his car and he wanted money to pay for the damage. Joe attacked Pupatee there and then, punching him and picking him up by the scruff of his neck to head-butt him, all in front of the man who stood there with a fearful expression on his face. He now saw what his son had warned him would happen.

The man shouted at Joe to stop, telling him that beating Pupatee would not pay for the car. Joe did stop, saving the rest of the beating for later. He went and found some money for the man who quickly left. Pupatee hadn't wanted his friend's father to come, but now he was there he didn't want him to leave. The minute the door closed, Joe's orders boomed through the house. 'Get up the stairs and strip. I'm going to give you a beating you'll never forget.' After the first ten licks with the flex wire, Pupatee was still not reacting, so Joe stopped for a moment. 'You turn a big man now,' he said, and then he brought his arm down with all his might, lashing him as if his life depended on it. Pupatee screamed now all right, calling out for Mama and Pops, half expecting in his delirium that they would come through the door and say: Enough is enough. How the next-door neighbours didn't report Pupatee's screaming he never knew.

Soon after he lost his job with Bill, Pupatee was made to get another, this time on a paper round, but when he started delivering to the wrong houses, he lost that job too. When Joe had finished beating him and calmed down a bit, he said, 'Boy, listen to me, go around all the

54

shops and ask them for a job, even if it is sweeping and mopping up and cleaning their toilets. Do you understand?'

'Yes, bredda,' Pupatee said quickly.

The next day he went around the greengrocers and he didn't have to ask many before one offered him a job. It was mentioning cleaning the toilets that did it. The greengrocer was a Greek man called Mr Memmet. Pupatee's duties included sweeping and mopping the shop, disposing of the empty boxes and keeping the cellar clean and tidy. Pupatee worked at weekends and sometimes after school and he got on fine with Mr Memmet.

Pupatee's place was out of the way at the back, but as time went on he would help Mr Memmet in the shop, and his friends like Flego would drop by. Flego lived with his two brothers, his sister and his father; his mother had gone off before Pupatee met him. His father was friendly but liked a drink, and so Flego was often left to his own devices.

One day, Pupatee was cleaning Mr Memmet's cellar when he came across a potato bag full of smaller bags of coins. Decimalisation had just been introduced, and there were hundreds of coins, five-pence, ten-pence and fifty-pence coins, all carefully bagged up. At first Pupatee didn't dare touch them, but the thought of all that money lying there began to prey on him. He was still not getting any pocket-money from Joe, so it was not long before he started to raid Mr Memmet's cellar.

Pupatee had to be careful, because as far as Joe was concerned his brother had no money, and if Joe ever discovered him with so much as a couple of pence jingling in his pocket he would have something to answer for. So he gave the new-found money to Flego for safe keeping. Sometimes Pupatee used it to buy better clothes than those supplied by Joe, but he only wore them when Joe wasn't around. At other times, when the coast was clear, the two boys would go down to the amusement arcades and play on the gambling machines. There were many of these arcades in Camberwell. They were warm, noisy places, with loud music and the chinking of coins, and multicoloured lights flashing in the gloom, full of young and old all busily trying their luck on the one-arm bandits and fruit machines. Pupatee and his friend were drawn to them like moths. There was one machine with a ledge that moved backwards and forwards; if you dropped your coin in and it was lucky enough to land at the very back, then on the next shove all the money at the front would fall to the player. If you weren't so fortunate, you could try pushing a bit of wire into the machine – but this was a tricky business, as the staff who ran the places were always on the look-out for wise guys. Sometimes Pupatee and Flego were lucky, but in the end they always lost more than they won.

Pupatee always looked forward to Saturdays, when Joe would send him down to Brixton to do the shopping. Brixton was full of life, and with all the black people there Pupatee's imagination would dance with memories of home. All sorts of Jamaican goods were sold in the markets and arcades. You could find mangoes there, and sugar-cane, water coconuts, yams, green bananas, sweet potatoes, coco and dasheen. Pupatee would often stop in delight, unable to believe his eyes, as he discovered some foodstuff he thought he had left behind for ever. When he finished his shopping, he would head over to sister Pearl's, and play with his nephews Richie and Roland. Roland, who was just a year older than him, he liked especially.

56

One morning, walking up from the shops towards sister Pearl's, Pupatee found Roland in the street and they sat on the steps outside the house, laughing and joking and soaking up the summer sunshine. 'That's Trigger and Boobs,' said Roland, pointing at two boys walking up the street towards them. As they approached, they began to shout at Roland, calling him names. Pupatee thought they were joking, but then Roland suddenly stood up and began to shout back at them, inviting them to follow up their words with action.

The boys were both bigger than Roland and they lost no time in advancing, saying, 'So wha, Roland, you a bad bwoy, you want fight?'

By this time Pupatee had realised it was serious. "We no need to fight,' he said, getting up.

'Shut up, you fat bastard,' said the one Roland had referred to as Trigger. His friend Boobs burst out laughing.

'Who you talking?' Pupatee asked.

'You, you fat blob. You think I'm frightened of you, you fat bastard?' Trigger and Pupatee were now only inches apart, eyeballing each other. Trigger was taller than Pupatee, but not as well built, and when Pupatee suddenly gave him an almighty push in the chest with both hands, he fell back and hit the floor like a sack of potatoes. Boobs came wading in flailing his arms, but Pupatee lashed out with a kick to the shin-bones and punched Boobs in the belly. Boobs ran back a few steps and stopped to recover his breath. He shouted, 'Come on, you big fat overgrown gorilla.'

Furious now, Pupatee charged at him and hit him at full pace, and a moment later Boobs was on his back. Meanwhile, Trigger had recovered and was shouting, 'Go on, Boobs, go on, me friend.' But Boobs got to his feet only to scarper down the street, with Trigger close behind him.

On another day in Brixton, Pupatee got into an argument with a lad named Scoby. He was smaller than Pupatee, but older and wiser, and when Pupatee made his usual challenge, Scoby looked at him cockily.

'You want to fight, no?' he asked. 'Wait, ah soon come back.' With that he left, and returned with his much bigger friend, Mike, dressed in Dr Marten boots, Levi Staypress jeans and a Fred Perry tennis shirt. His clothes alone were enough to make Pupatee feel inadequate. Close behind came Mike's older and even bigger brother, Big Youth.

'Let we see who we are going to beat up today,' laughed Big Youth.

'Come off it, lads,' said Roland, trying to save the situation. 'This is my uncle and he didn't mean no harm. Let's cool it, eh?'

The three boys stopped in their tracks. 'OK, Roland,' Scoby finally said. 'We'll forget it, but you'd better tell your uncle to watch who he gets cheeky with in the future.' And with that they left.

In all this time, Miss Utel only came back once to the house in Selborne Road. She turned up one day with Lena and Terry. Joe stared at her and said, 'What do you want?' Miss Utel tried running her hands through Joe's hair, but Joe jumped up and protested, saying he wasn't having any of that. He more or less told her to be on her way back to where she had come from, and shortly afterwards she and the children were gone.

When Miss Utel had been at home, Pupatee had listened to the names Joe called her – prostitute and whore and the like – and had been surprised that they made her cry. Joe wasn't hitting her, after all, and as

Pops used to say, 'cuss-cuss never bore hole in skin'. But now, alone in the house with Joe and subject to lashings from his vicious tongue, Pupatee began to see the power of words.

When a visitor come to the house and asked Joe, 'Oh, is this your little brother?' Joe would say something like, 'No, when my mother gave birth they took my brother and gave her that fucking afterbirth.' Some visitors would laugh, but others would look pained and tell Joe not to talk like that in front of Pupatee. On their own, Joe would continue with the same theme. 'You can't be my brother,' he would say. 'There must have been a mistake at the hospital, they must have switched babies to give Mama a little bastard like you.' Pupatee thought of his friend Jimmy, who had tried to show him that words could cool situations better than fists; and even his nephew Roland seemed to know that. But here in Selborne Road, Joe's words could break Pupatee's spirit just as his flex wire bruised the boy's flesh.

Once, for some reason Pupatee never knew, Joe took him on one of his driving jobs. He was dressed in his dark grey suit and cap with its British Rail badge on it. They drove in Joe's Vauxhall down to the depot where they picked up a long vehicle full of goods, and then set off through the city and out into the countryside. It seemed like hours later when they arrived at a big farm. Joe pulled in and they were told to leave the truck to be unloaded and go and have some breakfast. Pupatee followed Joe towards a building, thinking they were heading for a kitchen or a café, but as they drew closer Pupatee heard mooing and picked up a strong smell of flesh and blood.

Only when they entered the building did Pupatee

realise it was a slaughterhouse. In Jamaica, Pupatee had killed many small animals and had always wanted to join in the killing of the big fatted calves. But perhaps the years in England had softened him, or perhaps it was the difference between what had seemed natural in Jamaica and what seemed so unnatural here, for the place made Pupatee sick.

In front of them was a narrow channel, fenced off on either side with metal barriers. Inside was a row of cows. The channel was only just wide enough for a single line of them and they were being slowly driven forward, one at a time. As the animals neared the front, they began to smell and see the fate that awaited them, but there was nothing they could do. They could not turn around in the channel and they could not retreat, because there were more cows pushing from behind. They rolled their eyes in fear.

Pupatee watched, transfixed with horror, as the first animal reached the front gate. The gate opened, but the terrified creature pulled back in desperation, rearing up slightly and mooing in a horrible way. For a moment, the cows behind bunched up and the one in front managed to hold itself back, but then they were all driven forward and the first cow lurched into the death trap. It was held tightly in place, unable to move as it was finished off. A tool like a screwdriver was fired into its head, and it let out a dying cry and fell to its knees with a jolt. A metal shutter opened, and the corpse rolled out towards the waiting butchers, who set about skinning it with long knives. Steam rose as the beast's hide fell away from its flanks, and the hot smell of bone being sawn and the sound of flesh slapping against cold stone as other animals were carved up made Pupatee want to sick. He stared at the scene below, like a vision of hell, with tears in his eyes. Then the shutter closed and the next cow fell into the death trap. The whole place stank of stale blood.

'Yeah, take a good look,' Joe suddenly said. Pupatee had almost forgotten his brother was standing beside him. 'If you don't behave yourself this is where I'll bring you and toss you in there so you can go the same way as the cows.'

Pupatee had enough sense to realise that Joe didn't mean what he was saying. He was trying to frighten him to keep him in line, and there was a faint smile on his face, but the words had their effect. Pupatee knew he was no angel, and he deserved some of what Joe dished out to him. His brother was a proud man and an honest man and he wanted Pupatee to grow up better than he saw him doing. But the punishment Pupatee received from Joe was always out of proportion to the crime.

Despite the fear of a beating, Pupatee still regularly took out Joe's bike and went racing. Joe had never found out it was his bike that had caused the damage to that man's car. One sunny afternoon Pupatee and some other boys were careering through Camberwell when they came to a big hill that led down to Goose Green. Pupatee was in the lead, and he went tearing down that hill at a terrible pace. At the give-way sign at the bottom, he pulled desperately at the brakes and the bike went into a skid. Both Pupatee and his vehicle hit the ground and slid and tumbled down the road.

The bike wasn't badly damaged, but Pupatee was hurt. He couldn't feel or use his left hand. He took the bike home and then decided he should have his hand looked at, so he walked down to casualty at King's College Hospital, where he found out his wrist was broken. Bandaged up, he left the hospital sorrowfully.

After the last beating, he really didn't want to go home. He was already injured and it seemed to him that Joe was going to kill him sooner or later. In some ways he would have welcomed death, but he couldn't face it from Joe. So he turned away from home and walked around until he came to Ruskin Park. Eventually the keeper threw him out and locked the gate. But the park had seemed so pleasant, much more pleasant than what awaited him at home, that Pupatee simply climbed back over the wall.

The birds were singing their dusk songs, ducks were honking and squirrels were running up and down tree-trunks. Pupatee walked between horse-chestnut trees and sycamores and the overflowing flower-beds. The swings and slides were all empty, but he didn't feel like playing. He found a group of benches beside a bed planted with roses and, choosing one, lay himself down intent on spending the night there.

The night grew darker and Pupatee watched the stars come out, one by one. Although he was cold and in pain, he was overcome by that big night sky and for a while he did not sleep. He was content to just lie there, and soon he found himself relaxing. He was away from Joe. Slowly, his eyes began to close. He heard a sound and peering into the night he saw three shadowy figures coming towards the benches.

At first he thought they might be ghosts. Then he saw them sit down on a nearby bench and draw parcels wrapped in brown paper from their pockets and from inside their raggedy coats and jackets. They unscrewed the tops from their bottles and he listened to the slurps as they drank and laughed. Pupatee was frightened to death, for they were all big and rough looking. He lay still and prayed they wouldn't notice him, hoping that the morning would come soon with its sunlight and the safety of other people. He would even have welcomed being caught by the park keeper and given a few licks with the stick he used to pick up rubbish.

And then one of the tramps lifted his head and peered towards him. Excitedly, he touched one of his fellows and pointed at Pupatee. They all began to chatter and they stood up and silently began to creep towards Pupatee, hands outstretched. He closed his eyes, pretending to be asleep, and began to wish he was at home with Joe. Opening his eyes a crack, Pupatee saw them in the full moonlight. Their coats were ragged and their faces harsh and unshaven. They were so close they could have reached out and touched him. Then one put his hands in the air to stop the others.

'It's just a kid,' the tramp said. 'Leave him, he's just a kid.'

A sense of ease descended on Pupatee, dissolving after a moment into a faint feeling of regret, for part of him wished to be torn from his life. He would still have to face all his problems in the morning.

Pupatee was still nervous and lay absolutely still until eventually he must have fallen asleep, for suddenly the sun was up and the birds were singing away. The tramps were gone and the road by the park was busy with traffic. He opened his eyes wide and saw an aeroplane crossing the sky overhead. If only he could be on that plane, flying back to Jamaica, to Mama and Pops and Carl and Gamper, he thought. Then he got up and brushed the thought away. It was not often he turned his mind to Jamaica. He had left the island, left his family, left that part of him behind.

He walked out of the park and began to follow the roads at random, thinking he should go back to

Camberwell. And after a while he began to recognise the streets again and he realised where his mind had secretly been taking him: he was heading towards Brixton. Before long, he was walking through streets he knew well, making his way to Kellett Road and sister Pearl's house.

When he knocked on the pink door it was Roland who came to open it. 'Pupatee,' he said, with a look of horror and pity on his face. 'Ah weh you' been? Uncle Joe ah look everway fe you. Him ah go mad! If me was you, me would ah gone home already.'

'Me frighten him ah go beat me up,' Pupatee said.

'Den ah wha happen to you hand, man?'

Pupatee told him the whole story and Roland shook his head. 'Me tink Uncle Joe phone de Babylon,' he said. Just then, sister Pearl appeared and when she heard what Pupatee had done she asked why he hadn't come to her first.

'Joe ah go beat me,' Pupatee said simply. 'So me no want go home.'

Sister Pearl looked at him. She seemed concerned. Then she said, 'You hungry? Come, Roland mek you some brekfast. Go wash in ah de bathroom upstairs.'

From the bathroom, Pupatee heard her call Roland. 'Go look fe one ah you big T-shirts fe Pupatee wear, and bring down de dotty one him did ah wear fe wash.'

'Yea, Ma.'

Upstairs, in Roland's and Richie's room, Richie was reading a Superman comic. Pupatee went to the window and looked out into the garden. He felt warm and comforted by Sister Pearl's house.

'Yea man, Joe did come round vex, vex, vex!' Roland said when he came up.

'Me feel him ah go kill you, Pupatee,' Richie added.

Pupatee looked at Richie and wished that he was

him, safe and sound in his own family house, without a worry in the world.

Later that day, Joe came for Pupatee and took him back to Selborne Road. Sister Pearl made a half-hearted protest, but Joe was her older brother. The night Pupatee spent in the park had begun to change things, both in the eyes of his family, and somewhere deep inside himself.

Pupatee was still cooking for Joe and cleaning the house, but Joe was spending more and more time away in the evenings and at weekends. He would come home, change out of his uniform into his shirt and tie and suit and get in his Vauxhall Victor, looking cheerful and slick, and zoom away. Pupatee never really knew where he was going, though he assumed he must have had women. Joe didn't often bring friends to the house. He had lost his best friend Cecil when Miss Utel was still living at home. Cecil had visited the house a couple of times during the day, quite innocently as far as Pupatee knew, but Joe had gone mad, calling Miss Utel a whore and threatening Cecil.

When Joe was away, Pupatee was happy at home. He had the house to himself and didn't mind the darkness outside. He wasn't scared. He had grown up in Jamaica where there was no electricity and the nights were pitch black and full of strange noises.

Pupatee did what he could to have some sort of a life outside home. Though he had given up on the boxing, he signed on for school activities such as swimming and acting. Whenever possible, he headed down to Brixton to visit sister Pearl and Roland. He was even glad enough to work. He had lost his job at Mr Memmet's shop, and found a new one with another

65

greengrocer down the street. This one, Dave, had a beautiful young assistant, a brunette who always wore miniskirts no matter how cold it was. Dave never left any money lying around for Pupatee to take, but he was a kind employer and would give him as much overripe fruit as he could carry, which meant that some of Joe's shopping money could stay in Pupatee's pocket.

Every so often, Dave and his assistant would disappear into the back room and come out a little later looking exhausted. Pupatee was trusted to keep an eye on the shop, but he didn't know how to work the till, so when customers wanted to pay he would go out to the back and often caught Dave and his assistant tangled together.

One day, Dave was out back and the assistant told Pupatee to fetch him into the shop. Pupatee walked back and called out, 'Dave, your girlfriend wants you.' When the greengrocer came out into the shop full of customers, he gave Pupatee a stare, while the assistant had a look of horror on her face. When everyone had gone, including the assistant, Dave took him aside.

'Why did you call her my girlfriend, Pupatee?' he said. 'She is not my girlfriend.'

Pupatee turned away, thinking it better not to say anything. He began to pick up an empty box to take out into the back when Dave said, 'Tell you what, Pupatee, put a few things in that box for when you go home.'

'OK,' Pupatee said, and put a few bits of old fruit in as usual.

'Take more, Pupatee,' Dave said, and he started picking up fresh fruit and vegetables and filling up the box. 'Have this, and this,' he said. 'And take this. How about some of that over there?'

Pupatee was confused and beginning to get frightened. Joe would never believe he had been given all this. He would assume Pupatee had stolen it.

'Dave, you'll have to come and tell my brother you gave me all this,' Pupatee said.

'Look, Pupatee,' the greengrocer said after a pause. 'I need a younger boy to work for me now, because you are getting older and I don't want to pay higher wages.'

'It's OK, you can pay me anything.'

'No, Pupatee, a younger boy. I can give him a pound and no one can complain.' Then he took five pounds and stuffed it in Pupatee's pocket.

That night, Pupatee got a beating for losing the job.

What Joe inflicted on Pupatee, Pupatee in turn dealt out to the rest of the world, to other boys. He had become a bully, though he liked to think he never picked on kids smaller or younger than him, and that he used his strength and fierceness to defend people – which was sometimes, but not always, true. One way or another Pupatee had found that violence had a purpose. It won respect and position. He had crossed boundaries, gone further than he should, and found that nothing terrible happened. He supposed it was the same with Joe. Joe beat him and the heavens didn't fall. Pupatee beat up other boys and stole money and the world went on. So they both continued.

One day, in the school playground, two white boys and a black boy from another school walked past and began making comments about some of the girls through the fence. Pupatee strode over to see what was happening and told the boys to cool themselves.

'Who you ah talk to?' the black boy said.

'You,' answered Pupatee. 'Leave them alone.'

'Is you gal or something, no?'

67

'No, it don't matter what they are to me, just stop upsetting them.'

'So what you going to do bout it if we no left de gal dem?' the black boy challenged.

By this time the whole school was backed up behind Pupatee, shouting at him to tell them to piss off, and the next moment the boys had challenged him to a fight outside school. Pupatee said he would see them later.

The news spread so quickly that the teachers soon heard and gave out warnings against fights. But that day in the wood and metal workshop Pupatee secretly fashioned a knife, intending to take it with him. Another boy talked him out of it, so Pupatee hid the knife.

When he and his friends reached the school gate, Pupatee saw the three boys walking down the street towards them. The black boy approached and asked if Pupatee was ready to fight. Before Pupatee could even answer, he slashed something sharp towards him. Pupatee pulled back and reached up, half expecting to feel an open wound and blood pouring out. Fortunately, the boy hadn't really aimed to cut him, but Pupatee was fuming and turned and marched back into the school to get his knife, all eleven inches of it. With the knife in his hand, he ran back out towards the gate. Fortunately, the three boys were gone. But Pupatee was so full of anger that if he had caught them no thoughts of the police or gaol, or even Joe, would have prevented him from using that knife.

Every Friday afternoon, two of the teachers would take a group of kids from the school to the Cockpit Theatre in the West End to take part in drama workshops. Pupatee loved the acting and the chance to get away and meet new kids.

One Friday morning, before leaving for work, Joe gave Pupatee five pounds and told him to buy some white paint so he could start redecorating the front of the house that weekend. Pupatee knew that by the time he finished at the Cockpit the shops would be closed, so he decided to rush out and get the paint before school. He would be a bit late for his first class, but that was better than missing drama.

As soon as the shops opened, Pupatee ran across the road and got the paint. On the way back, he thought about helping Joe to paint the front of the house. It was the kind of thing Pupatee liked doing. Joe had recently begun to do up the house a bit, buying a new coffee-table, television and settee. His prize purchase was a bright green carpet in the living-room.

Pupatee rushed into the house and put the tin on the mantelpiece. But no sooner had he let go of it to turn away than there was a terrible crash. He looked round and to his horror saw the tin, lid off, spilling white paint all over Joe's prize carpet. 'Oh God, have mercy, he'll kill me,' Pupatee said out loud. He picked up what was left of the paint and set to work on the carpet with paint stripper, turps, paraffin, liquid soap and anything else he could think of. He cleaned that carpet for dear life, once, twice and three times. And then there was no more to be done: the carpet was permanently stained with a horrible mixture of white paint and the various substances he had applied. He was sure he would get the beating of his life that night.

Pupatee took his bag and headed out to school – very late now, but he didn't care. He was deep in depression. He didn't smile or laugh once. He felt lonely and unloved. The whole school must have told him to cheer up, but he was too heavy with the thoughts in his head.

A couple of boys pressed him to tell them what was

the matter and when Pupatee did they failed to understand. 'Don't be silly,' they said. 'Is that all? You're looking as if the world is coming to an end. Cheer up, mate.'

As the day wore on and the time when Pupatee knew Joe would come home and see the stained carpet drew closer, he became more and more downcast. At the end of school, the teachers took the drama group off to the Cockpit; Pupatee never enjoyed an acting session less. Finally came the moment when the teachers told them all to go home. The other kids piled out laughing and talking, ready for the weekend, wanting to get home to where their mothers would have their tea waiting for them.

Pupatee got on the bus with his white friend Danny, who lived not far from him in Camberwell. Danny was weird looking. He walked with his feet pointing out, and he had a peculiar, skinny body. But the oddest thing about him was his face, which seemed much too big for the rest of him. When he laughed, which he did wholeheartedly, his face would become even bigger, his smile pushing out his cheeks, and his chin pointing down towards his chest. Not that Pupatee minded. On the way home Danny asked Pupatee what was wrong, and when Pupatee tried to explain he didn't put him down. He seemed sympathetic.

While the bus worked its way through the crowded streets of the city, Pupatee thought about what lay ahead. And by the time they reached Camberwell he had made up his mind.

'Danny,' he said, 'I can't go home, I got to avoid this beating. I canna take no more. Can I come round your house?'

'Yes,' said Danny, without hesitation. 'You can come round.'

'Danny, can I *stay* at your house?' pleaded Pupatee.

'I don't see why not, if you ask my mum and dad.'

When they reached Danny's flat, Danny immediately blurted out the story to his mother, and just as he was asking if Pupatee could stay the weekend, Danny's dad arrived home.

'Is this true?' Danny's parents asked Pupatee.

'He is going to beat me bad.'

'OK,' Danny's mum said. 'You can stay here for the weekend, but on Monday you must leave."

'Thank you, Mrs—'

'Madge, you can call me Madge,' and she gave him a big smile and a motherly wink. And Danny's dad took Pupatee's hand, shaking it hard, and told him to call him Tom. For the first time all day Pupatee felt like smiling, so he did.

'Are you hungry?' Madge asked.

'We're starving, Mum,' said Danny.

They ate dinner and then Tom, Danny and Pupatee went to watch television while Madge busied herself washing up and ironing and tidying the place.

'Pupatee,' Danny said after a while, 'Dad knows some good jokes, don't you, Dad? Tell us one, Dad, go on.' Tom laughed and told a few jokes. They didn't seem very funny to Pupatee, but he was glad to be with them, and put on a good show of smiling and laughing until it was time for bed. There was only one bed in Danny's room, so he lay at one end and Pupatee lay at the other. Despite the squeeze, Pupatee slept like a log.

After breakfast the next morning they lounged about the house for a while and then decided to go out for a walk through Danny's estate. It was uneventful until they ran across a group of other kids, some younger than them and some older, who all started pointing and whispering. Then one of the older boys shouted out that Danny shouldn't be around there.

'Why can't I come here?' Danny shouted back.

'You fucking well know why, Danny,' the oldest boy said aggressively. 'The things you do to little girls.'

Pupatee stood there, his mouth hanging open. He didn't understand what was going on. The boy came over to him and said, 'No disrespect to you, mate, but I wouldn't hang around with him if I was you. He is a child-sex case. Lots of people hate him round here for what he's done.'

Pupatee still didn't know what was going on, but he could sense that Danny must have done something pretty bad as he had now turned as red as a cherry and made no attempt to defend himself. And then a woman leaned out of the window of one of the flats and started shouting. 'Get that dirty little evil bastard away from my children,' she yelled.

'See, Danny, you'd better clear off,' said one of the kids. With that, Danny was gone as quickly as he was a greyhound chasing a rabbit at the track. Pupatee stood there staring all around, not knowing what to do.

By now, the woman from the window had come down. 'That boy will get you into serious trouble, young man,' she said. 'Do you know what that dirty sod done? He put his hand down my little girl's knickers.' She pointed to a girl of about five. 'I'll kill him if I catch him round here.'

Pupatee found Danny back at the flat. 'You didn't have to run, Danny,' he told him when he got there. 'I'd have helped you if any of them had started anything.' Though Pupatee wasn't sure he would have. Danny put his finger to his lips and dragged his friend outside, but Madge appeared almost immediately.

'What's wrong?' she asked, narrowing her eyes.

'Nothing, Mum.'

'Why have you come back then? You only went out a little while ago.'

'We just . . . we just felt like coming back, that's all.'

Madge looked down sternly at them. She had just got out of the bath and was wearing a long dressing-gown, with a towel wrapped around her head. 'All right then, Danny,' she said. 'But seeing as you're home you can go and tidy that mess of a bedroom of yours.'

As Danny went to his room, Madge pulled Pupatee into the sitting-room.

'Pupatee, I know you and Danny are mates,' she said. 'But I don't want you to lie for him. Now, what happened out there today? Tell the truth, Pupatee.' She held Pupatee's arms and looked at him as if life itself depended on him telling the truth.

'It my fault, Madge,' Pupatee said. 'I wanted to walk that way and Danny was only following. And then we ran into these other kids.'

'Go on.'

Pupatee hesitated, but then he thought he'd better do as she asked. Even saying the words he'd heard the kids and woman speak made him feel ashamed, as if he was dirtying himself.

Madge nodded at him. 'I'm glad you told me the truth, Pupatee. There's something I think you should know, too. Danny was accused of touching some kids round the back of the flats and it seems there was some truth to it. Where there's smoke there's fire. I've told him I'll kill him if it happens again. I'll call the police myself next time.'

Madge stopped talking suddenly as Danny came in. She went out, giving Pupatee a pleading look. Danny was immediately down Pupatee's earhole. 'What did she ask you? What did you tell her?' Pupatee told him he'd said nothing.

The subject never came up again and Danny's parents treated Pupatee well. They gave the boys money to go to the pictures with enough over for hot dogs, drinks and ice-cream. Back at the flat, Danny's mum cooked up big meals and treated Pupatee like her own, always making sure he had enough. Pupatee even began to enjoy Danny's dad's boring jokes. It was so friendly in that house Pupatee thought he could have stayed there for ever.

Eventually Monday morning came round. Pupatee said goodbye to Madge and Tom and thanked them for the weekend. But after all their kindness to him, he did something really heartless: he didn't know why, but just before he left he stole a lighter from on top of the television and hid it in his pocket. Then he and Danny trooped off to school.

The day began without trouble, but in the afternoon Pupatee was called into the office of the headmaster, Mr Bishop. With his big white beard he looked like Captain Bird's Eye. Pupatee found sister Pearl with the headmaster. She asked where Pupatee had been all weekend, and said Joe had called the police and everyone had been so worried.

Pupatee told her everything and swore he would not go back to Selborne Road with Joe. 'OK, then,' Pearl said eventually. 'You can come by me after school and then you and me and Mr H will sort it out.' Pupatee was so delighted with this that he was on top of the world that day, showing off his new lighter and laughing with everyone, as happy now as he had been unhappy on the Friday before. Deep down he knew he shouldn't have stolen the lighter, but it was too late to give it back, so he forgot about his crime and enjoyed himself.

That night, Joe came round to sister Pearl's and

leaped at him and started to beat Pupatee before he even had a chance to explain himself. Sister Pearl screamed and shouted at him to leave Pupatee alone. Now she had seen with her own eyes what Joe did.

'Come on,' Joe growled at Pupatee. 'We're going home.' Conditioned to obey Joe, a part of Pupatee told him to stand up and follow him. But he stood firm and said nothing. Joe gave him a final glare. 'Don't ever tell anyone we are brothers,' he yelled. Then he slammed the door and was gone.

4

Brixton Front Line

A few evenings after Pupatee arrived in Brixton, Roland took him out to the Blue Lagoon café. This was run by Mr C, a black man, and Mrs J, a white lady, who were both loved and respected by everybody. The tables and chairs were laid out in neat rows and on each table were pots of hot pepper sauce, vinegar, salt, and pepper. To walk into the café was to enter a world of wonderful smells of Caribbean cooking.

The Blue Lagoon was one of the favourite hang-outs for the local West Indian kids. Many of them were about the same age as Pupatee – thirteen or fourteen – but though they were smaller than him (he had grown into a bulky boy) they seemed older. They were all dressed in up-to-the-minute clothes like Levi's, Wrangler's or Lee Cooper's jeans – some flares, some bell-bottoms – with Fred Perry T-shirts, Ben Shermann and Brutus shirts, crombie coats, and leather or suede jackets, all of which made Pupatee mistakenly think they were the children of rich families. They seemed to him to have a maturity beyond their years. They flashed money and played table football confidently, and Pupatee felt very self-conscious among them.

Suddenly, one of the lads looked up from the football table and stared at him.

'Oh! Wait, no,' the boy said to his friends. 'That guy over deh with Roland give we a wicked beating one day, eh Trigger?'

'Blood claat, ah him yes, ah him, same one, Boobs.'

Boobs and Trigger, Pupatee thought, the same Boobs and Trigger he had fought once in Brixton. Lots of the kids had stopped talking and were now watching to see what would happen. Boobs and Trigger walked over and asked if he wanted to start where they had left off in the street. But there was no threat in their voices and Pupatee smiled back and shrugged his shoulders. In a moment, they were all smiling, and Pupatee was being bought a drink and a bun with cheese. Soon he had been introduced to the other boys. Mike and Big Youth, with whom he had also nearly fought on a separate occasion, were there too.

'What your name?' someone asked.

'Tee,' he said. This was a name he had sometimes been called in Camberwell. He was growing up now, and it was time to leave the childish Pupatee behind.

As he made all these new friends, time seemed to fly by. Mrs J walked out of the kitchen carrying a tray of ackee and saltfish and a plate of salad, and Tee suddenly realised how hungry he was. Roland must have had the same feeling, because he beckoned him to leave.

'Mum must have cooked dinner by now,' he said. 'Hey,' he called out to the others, 'later, me gone ca me ah get hungry, star.'

'All right, me breddren.'

'Boobs, Trigger.'

'Later,' they said. Then they asked Tee if he would still be around and Tee replied happily, 'Yeah man, later!'

Roland and Tee left the café and as they were crossing the road Roland pointed out a short, stocky black guy: 'Yow, Smurphy!' It was another friend. Brixton seemed full of young West Indians, and Roland apparently knew them all. They stopped and talked for a while, and then they headed back home for dinner. The meal was just being shared out when they arrived, and after quickly washing their hands Roland and Tee sat down to a delicious meal of Caribbean stew peas and rice.

Having lived alone with Joe, and done the cooking himself, it was a real treat for Tee to be part of a family again, sitting down with friendly faces and seeing the food arrive as if by magic. Within days he was happily used to the pattern of this new life. After dinner, the kids would help with the washing-up and then settle down for an evening in front of the television. Tee had never felt so happy.

He and Roland were free to come and go almost as they liked, as long as they were in before eleven. Roland loved music, and whenever possible they would head for a youth club or disco or party. One of their favourite clubs was a place called Shepherd's, which was open Monday, Wednesday and Friday evenings until half past ten. The gatherings here were mostly black, although there were always some whites and Asians.

In those days, youth clubs like Shepherd's were mostly about dancing, and many of them held dance competitions. Tee was big and good at fighting, but Roland was slim and athletic and a star dancer. The dance of the time was a quicksilver style they called shuffling, and pairs of dancers would compete against each other to shuffle their feet faster and more brilliantly than each other. As the music beat faster, they would try out more and more dazzling moves until one of them would produce a step so quick and daring that he would be declared the winner. Often this was Roland.

If he was giving his feet a rest, Roland would be disc jockeying, a microphone in his hand. Music was his life, and when he and Tee weren't at the clubs or roaming the streets or watching *Lost in Space* or *The Untouchables* on television, they would be upstairs where Roland would sing the latest song he had written.

At home in Pearl's and Mr H's house, Tee was always well behaved, polite and honest like Roland and Richie. But once out on the streets he was a free spirit. Previously he had always been running back home to cook and clean for Joe or work at his latest task, but now he had more free time to spend out on the streets, or at Shepherd's or the Blue Lagoon café or other hang-outs. And the boys he became friendly with were those he had fought with over the years, teenagers like Big Youth, Scoby, Trigger, Mike Winston, Fritz, Chance and Boobs, who were already smoking and drinking and trying to follow in the footsteps of the older youths they saw on the streets of Brixton.

Roland didn't like this new turn in Tee's life and would often warn him to be careful with these lads. But Tee would just tell Roland to relax. Pearl saw Tee only for what he was at home. If she had known the circle her little brother Pupatee was running with, she might have done something. But she didn't, and so it went on. As for what Joe would have done – well, he was completely out of the picture now.

Of course, this little firm had certain expectations, and with the unfashionable clothes Joe had bought him from the cheapest shops, Tee was sadly failing to meet their dress code. Even his best shoes were just an old pair of Joe's winkle-pickers, which were the laughing stock of Brixton. The boys all wore mohair and staypress material, makes like Harrington, Ben Shermann and Brutus. Pearl didn't have much money, but Tee pleaded with her, and after several weeks of saving and promising, she took him down to Temple's shop on Railton Road and bought him a two-tone suit, reddish from one angle, blueish from another.

They went home and Tee put on the suit. He swanked out to Shepherd's and when friends told him how good he looked he felt on top of the world. But when he found Big Youth and Boobs and the gang, they all started laughing. It was Big Youth who finally spoke.

'Nice, Tee,' he said. 'You're a decade out, but it's all right.'

Tee had been in England nearly five years. He was fourteen and almost as big as a man. But England still felt to him like a fairy-tale land, a place he didn't belong to, where his future was too fantastical to worry about. Something would happen once upon a time and he had no more say over it than he did over the behaviour of giants or beanstalks. And if he didn't know where he was going, it didn't bother him. Life to him was what he made of it at that instant.

Later, all he would be able to recall was that he was easily excited, easily drawn into mischief, easily led astray. He believed that this was the way of everybody.

Living with Joe, he had had every excuse for behaving badly. He was alone with a brutal brother. If he was bad, then he was beaten into badness. But in fact, Joe's beatings had kept him disciplined. He

80

borrowed Joe's bike, and stole small amounts of money, and got into fights. But he did what almost every kid does. The friends he had in Camberwell were never into more than petty mischief. And he would have backed away from anything more serious both for fear of Joe, and also, in a funny way, out of respect for him. Joe was the most honest man in the world. If he had found a twenty-pound note on the pavement, Joe would have handed it in to the police.

Now that he was in Brixton with Pearl and her family, Tee was the happiest and most comfortable he had been since leaving Jamaica. By rights he should have settled down and learned from their honest influence. But he was so used to Joe's harsh discipline that without it there was nothing to control him. Love and kindness weren't enough to keep him on the straight and narrow. Or perhaps it was simply his own nature. But while Roland worked at his music and his education, Tee would sneak out to busy himself with less honourable pursuits. When he wasn't nestled in the bosom of Pearl's family, he would be standing about on the street corners of Brixton with his new-found friends, Scoby, Big Youth and all the others. They were more than friends, they were a gang, christened the Herbies after the weed they smoked. It had been coined as a dismissive term, in reference to their degenerate ways. But they took it as a compliment, and adopted the name.

That first summer in Brixton the trees were bright and green, and the blue sky was filled with birds flying low and singing sweet melodies. Mothers and fathers and all their children filled Brockwell Park and the open-air swimming-pool. At weekends, sound systems were set up and sections of the park were packed with people dancing, playing, laughing, eating and listening to the sounds of Sir Lord Coxon, Duke Reid, Sofrano B, Duke Vin, and TWJ. There were always thousands of people at those dances, black and white, and the Herbies would be there, spreading out and having fun.

One day, in the school holidays, the Herbies decided to cycle down to Battersea Park. It was the same old problem: Tee didn't have a bike, so he had to stay behind. It was no use bothering Pearl to buy him one, as she found it hard enough clothing and feeding him. But when one of the Herbies said he was going to nick a front wheel to replace the buckled one on his bike, Tee's mind was made up. A few days later, he was in Peckham when he saw a brand-new, ten-gear bike leaning against a wall. Without a moment's hesitation, he jumped on and rode away. In a flash he was in Brixton, where the Herbies stared open mouthed in admiration at his slick new vehicle, eyes popping out of their heads. Tee was bursting with pride.

'You'd better get it painted before the Old Bill sees it, mate,' said Big Youth.

'Well, I can't take it home,' Tee said. 'Could you look after it and perhaps put a bit of paint on it for me?'

'No problem,' said Big Youth.

It was nearly time for dinner, so Tee left the bike and went home all excited. The following day, he knocked on Big Youth's door and asked for his bike.

'It was best to give it some changes,' Big Youth said. Tee stared in horror at the bare frame he was holding, the chain drooping off like a greasy necklace.

'What happened?' he said, fury rising inside him.

Tee listened while Big Youth blamed Mike, and Mike blamed Big Youth. He turned from one to the other, not knowing who to blame, and soon the other Herbies turned up and the story was told all over again – how Tee had found this beautiful new racing bike and given it to Big Youth and Mike to look after, and how the next morning there it was, all stripped. Everyone laughed and laughed. Tee thought it was a crime, but the others seemed to think it was a big joke. When the story had been told for the umpteenth time, Tee simply took the frame and threw it in his back yard, where it stayed while the Herbies continued to ride down to Battersea without him. But he kept one of those bike spanners in his pocket, and a few days later, when he saw a bike chained up by the front wheel in a side street in Herne Hill, he checked to see no one was around and then took off the back wheel. At every moment as he walked away he was sure he would hear a sudden cry of 'Thief!' but before long he was home and fixing the wheel on to his frame. Soon he was out hunting the streets for a front wheel. It wasn't long before he came across a bike chained by its back wheel so out came his spanner and then he had a two-wheeled bike. Big Youth gave him a seat and brakes, and he went to the bike shop and bought some second-hand cow handlebars. He stripped and sandpapered the whole bike down to silver – frame, handlebars, brakes and all. The next time the Herbies ventured out to Battersea, Tee tagged along with them on his silver bike, enjoying the fun.

In Battersea Park, they would head for the steep, rough hill. At first Tee was frightened, but he steeled himself and flew down it, gaining respect from the other Herbies for his fearlessness. On the days they didn't go down to Battersea, they just hung around the neighbourhood, riding their bikes and trying out tricks. Soon Tee could ride with his hands behind his back like everyone else.

They all wore Levi's jeans and Dr Marten boots. Even Tee soon had a pair of Levi's, but he was desperate for some DMs. Eventually, he resorted to asking sister Pearl if she could help. She promised to see what she could do, and a few days later she took him out shopping. She couldn't afford Dr Martens, but bought him some cheaper monkey boots. They seemed perfectly good to Tee, but the next day when he went out he was the laughing stock of the whole gang. Monkey boots were simply not Dr Martens – though in the end, Big Youth told him not to worry. 'Boots are boots,' he said, and that was the end of that.

One Saturday, some of the Herbies said they were heading off to the West End. Tee asked what they were going to do. They didn't tell him, but said he could go along with them. So off he went on the tube with Big Youth, Mike, Trigger, Boobs and Johnny. They didn't need any money, as they never paid on the tube. They would simply walk past the ticket collectors. Sometimes the collectors wouldn't even notice them walking through in the crowd, and if they did notice and call after the boys for their tickets, they would simply ignore them and walk on out into the street.

They arrived in the West End and were soon lost in the Saturday afternoon crowds. Tee had not often been to this part of London, and he was dazzled by all the shops and fashionable clothes. Everything was so busy. The pavements were packed with people going about their business – shoppers, tourists, couples with pushchairs and gaggles of noisy teenage girls, chattering, laughing, stopping to look at cinema posters or in shop windows. Others were pushing past in a hurry to get somewhere. There were people hopping on and off buses in the slow-moving traffic; the lights changed from orange to red to green and back again, and pedestrians darted between the cars as their drivers honked impatiently. The sight and smell of the food being served at the little hot-dog and hamburger stands made Tee's mouth water. There was so much to take in, and people wove around him as he trailed open mouthed after his friends.

Tee followed Big Youth and the others into a clothes shop, where they all wandered about, admiring the expensive clothes. When they left, they headed for a quiet side street, a few blocks away from the shop. There, Big Youth and the rest started pulling out shirts and trousers from bags they had been carrying with them, taking off their coats to reveal brand new jackets beneath. Tee was amazed and impressed.

It was not long before Tee was joining in the shop-lifting. If anyone needed new clothes, it was him, because Pearl couldn't afford to buy him much. So the next time the Herbies set off to steal clothes, he went prepared.

It was a Saturday. They split up into small groups so they would not look so suspicious. Tee went with Big Youth and Mike. He was wearing a long coat with a couple of plastic bags in the pockets. In his hand he held a big carrier bag with a shirt already in it, to look as if he was shopping.

Big Youth, Mike and Tee walked into a shop where there was only one assistant. He came over to them right away. 'Can I help you?' he said, smiling at them.

'Is it OK if we just have a look around?' asked Big Youth in his most polite voice.

'Certainly, sir, be my guest. What kind of clothes are you looking for?'

'A suit,' Big Youth said.

'Suits are over this side. If you'll come with me, I'll show them to you.'

While Big Youth and the shop assistant busied themselves with the suits, Mike and Tee headed over to some beautiful Prince-of-Wales-checked jackets. Tee tried one on and it fitted him perfectly. He glanced around. The shop assistant was not looking. So he pulled off the tags and threw his coat over the top, buttoning it up tight. He turned to the mirror, and saw that he looked just as cool as when he had entered the shop. He couldn't believe he had stolen such an expensive jacket.

Big Youth and the assistant were still occupied, so Tee found some nice trousers in his size and as he was stuffing two pairs into his big carrier bags, he heard Big Youth say to the assistant, 'Just got to go and change some money at the change bureau and I'll be back to buy that suit.' With that, they left the shop and a block or so away, Tee took off the jacket and put it in his bag. They were really shopping now!

In the next shop, Tee stalled the assistant while Big Youth and Mike both went to town. After a while, he heard one of them say, 'Come on, Mum and Dad will be waiting for us.' This was the green light for them to go.

'Are you open late tonight?' Tee asked the assistant.

'Yes, we are, sir.'

'I'll be back later,' he said. 'When I'm sure what I want.' And they walked out. He couldn't believe it was so easy.

Tee was jealous when he saw all the gear Big Youth and Mike had nicked in such a short time – jackets, shirt, trousers and a pullover. Even so he was pleased with his first effort.

They took the tube back to Brixton and went straight from the station to the Blue Lagoon café. It was packed with locals playing table football and pinball, eating, watching television and talking. Tee was still carrying his bag, and some of the other lads, who knew where they had been, asked to see what he had got. Tee took out the jacket and saw again what a beauty it was. Its brown, white and gold checks dazzled his eyes. Breezely nearly popped out of his head with jealousy.

'Let's have a wear,' he pleaded.

'You must be mad,' said Tee. He'd learned his lesson over the bicycle.

At home, Tee sneaked into the house and up the stairs past sister Pearl who was in the kitchen with Selena. Richie and Roland were upstairs drawing pictures of comic heroes like the Hulk, Spiderman and Captain America.

'Wha appen Tee?' they said.

'Wha you mean?' he replied.

'Wha dat you have deh in you bag?' Roland asked.

'Some things me stole.'

He showed them his new clothes and Roland looked them over enviously.

'They're nice,' he said. 'But you'd better watch yourself and what you're doing.'

'I'm all right, man, you no see me never get catch.'

'But you may one day,' Richie said.

'Well, me didn't today, so forget it.'

The following Friday night, when Tee wore the jacket to Shepherd's, the whole club must have commented on how nice it looked and Tee's head was soon swollen. Boobs was there, with his half-caste girlfriend, Gee. So were Big Youth and Mike, both dressed extra sharp. When Gee's friend told Tee how smart the jacket was, he went into the men's room to look in the full-length mirror. 'Boy, Tee,' he thought, 'you look wicked.' That night he went into the men's room again and again to admire himself in the mirror.

Tee and the Herbies didn't go stealing every day. Sometimes they would just hang about on the streets playing childish games, and nobody seeing them would have dreamed that they were capable of anything criminal. And sometimes Tee stayed at home with Roland and Richie. But he had found an easy way to get nice things, and once he had a taste of the good life, he wanted more. He never stopped to think what it might do to sister Pearl, though he had enough sense to hide his activities from her.

In those days, up from the Herbies was a gang of older, wiser, badder boys called the Rebels, led by a very advanced and educated villain known simply as Rebel. These boys were always dressed from head to foot in the best clothes, and had the most dazzling girlfriends. Rebel and his sidekick, Buzzer, even drove their own cars, and they were always loaded down with pocket-fuls of cash.

Tee idolised Rebel, Buzzer and the rest and wanted nothing so much as to be one of them. He could think of no better life. Even if one of them was sent off to borstal for a crime, his girls and friends would carry on talking about him non-stop, and the day he came home the welcoming laid on for the returning hero would make Tee wish it was him just getting out.

The Rebels' uniform was a long, thick, green and silver checked coat, and at clubs and parties they always stood out. They were not to be messed with. Tee was a fast-growing boy, well mannered and eager to make friends, and it was not long before he and a few others of the Herbies began to get noticed by the Rebels. Eventually, Big Youth or Trigger or one of the Herbies discovered the shop that sold the Rebel coats and it wasn't long before they'd all managed to steal one.

The next club night, when they wore their coats to Shepherd's, the Rebels asked them where they had got them. They seemed upset and told the younger boys to take it easy and not go to the shop too often and hot it up for them. But before long, all the bad boys who saw themselves as future Rebels had got themselves a coat and slowly but surely the Rebels grew into one big family, drawing members from several gangs all over Brixton. Most of the members were from Jamaican families, but there were also an Indian (they called him Coolie), a couple of Chinese-looking West Indians, a few Greeks, and some whites. What made you a Rebel or a Herbie wasn't the colour of your skin, but growing up in Brixton and the friends you had.

The Rebels made their money by stickdropping – pickpocketing. Big Youth and Mike and Tee soon began to try this for themselves. A couple of the older boys gave them a quick lesson, showing them how to distract people and then dip into their pockets using their first two fingers like pincers. Later, Tee came to learn there were many pickpocketing tricks, but the use of the fingers like pincers was the main art. They had to be strong – good pickpockets would exercise their fingers, and Tee even heard of some who deliberately broke and then fixed their index fingers so they made better pincers for dipping – people could not feel your hand in their pockets and handbags.

It wasn't long before Big Youth, Mike and Tee set out for the West End to try some stickdropping for themselves. Walking through the crowded streets, packed with shoppers and tourists, they saw the world in a new light. Handbags and pockets drew them like moths to a light bulb. They went into a busy clothes shop. Tee noticed a man who had taken off his jacket, which was draped over the back of a chair, and was trying on something in the changing-room. Tee crept over and quietly dipped into the jacket pocket and came out of the changing-room, and Big Youth, Mike and Tee quickly slipped away.

Out in the streets, they opened up the wallet. At first they thought it was crammed with nice brown tenners, but on closer examination the notes were found to be some strange money. Tee took in Mike's long face and Big Youth's silence, and he walked away saying, 'That's rubbish money.' They didn't follow him and he went off on his own. This time he tried the real thing, pickpocketing from a jacket a man was wearing and then walking away innocently, as if he was another tourist. It was a good touch, and when he got back to Brixton and saw Big Youth and Mike he excitedly showed them his ball of five-pound and ten-pound notes. To his surprise, they showed him an even bigger ball of tenners. They had known all along that the money in the wallet was simply foreign and could be changed at any bureau along Oxford Street.

'We were going to give you some, mate,' Big Youth said. 'But since you've made a fortune yourself, we'll all just go and buy some drink and ciggies and have a good smoke.'

For all Tee's venturing with the Herbies into petty crime, he still had a sense of honour, a feeling for right and wrong. It was OK to steal from wealthy tourists or clothes shops which could afford the loss, but he would never allow anyone weak or defenceless to be picked on. He had his own code of honour.

One holiday this sense of honour was nearly the end of him. He found himself at the fun-fair in Peckham, spending his ill-gotten gains. The place was packed with people having fun, eating candyfloss, throwing balls at coconuts and queuing for all the rides. Tee had just finished on the bumper cars when he saw a bit of wood flying through the air. Fortunately, it missed everyone. But a moment later, he saw people running to one end of the fair where a crowd was standing in a circle. He pushed his way in and saw four of the fun-fair men, armed with various weapons, beating up two girls. Tee knew them. They were Valerie and Esther.

'You can't do that,' he shouted, walking forward. The men looked up and without hesitating came straight for him. For a moment Tee saw them, sledgehammers and pickaxe handles held up, and then a blow caught him and he fell to the ground. The next thing he saw was a sledgehammer coming down towards his head, and as he scrambled away he saw it smashing into the earth beside him. His eyes passed over the crowd and he caught sight of people he recognised from school, but no one stepped forward to help.

The next blow landed on him, and the next. Tee tried his old trick of playing dead, but the blows kept coming. He rolled away and tried to shelter at the feet of the crowd, but they only moved away, screaming and fearful for themselves. And then he was staring up at the beautiful lights and shapes moving in the sky. There was music and excited screaming and laughter in the distance. He realised he was still at the fair, looking up at the big wheel. He was being put on a stretcher. And then he passed out again.

'How is he, doctor?' he heard a voice saying. It was Pearl.

'He stands a fifty–fifty chance,' a strange voice said. 'He took some severe blows to the head, as well as the body.'

He drifted back into unconsciousness. Later he was told he had been asleep for several days. Then, one morning, he woke up complaining that he was hungry.

91

He smelt food coming closer and tried to look, but he couldn't. He couldn't see! For a moment he thought he was blind. But then he found that if he forced his eyelids open with his fingers, he could see a bit. The food was on a shiny tray which he held up to his face like a mirror. He screamed and threw down his food when he saw what they had done to him.

For days he lay there consumed with violent hatred, contemplating what he would do to those fair workers when he caught up with them. The local newspaper had actually reported that he had been beaten to death, and after that gangs from Brixton went up to Peckham to find the fairground employees. For several days, Peckham was afire with fighting.

Many people came to visit him. Of course Pearl was there, and Roland and Richie, all of his relatives. Even Joe came once to check up on him – with all his beatings, he had never hurt his younger brother this bad. He didn't stay long. Friends also came, and people he didn't know were friends. At school, his worst enemy was a white boy called Roy. But almost every day, Roy would come to the hospital. 'Don't worry, Tee,' he would say. 'You'll make it, and when you get better and come out we'll go and get those dirty bastards.' Tee loved Roy for that.

When Tee finally returned to his school in Peckham, he got a standing ovation in front of the whole assembly. The head teacher called him out to the front. 'Just look at him, boys and girls, scarred and in bandages simply for trying to protect two girls.'

Slowly he recovered, and before long he was hanging out with the Herbies and the Rebels again, following them wherever they went. Often they would go to the pictures, to the Odeon, the ABC or the Classic Picture House, nicknamed the Bug House. They would stand

92

in the queue, pretending to be eighteen. If they were stopped at the box office, they would find some other way of getting in. One day at the Odeon, thwarted at the door, Big Youth led them round the back to an open window. 'Let's climb in here,' he said. It was such a small window that Tee thought he was joking, but everyone managed to squeeze through until only Tee was left. He pulled himself up and got his head, an arm and a shoulder in. But he was bigger than the rest of them, and he couldn't get any further. What was worse, he couldn't go back, either. He was stuck. All his friends were now in fits of laughter, which soon attracted the doorman, who came and gave him a good hiding while he was still stuck fast. For weeks after, he was the laughing stock of the entire gang.

From then on, they made it their business to find easier ways of getting into the cinemas. They found a side door at the Odeon which could be opened with a good hard kick. One of them would kick and then they would all rush in. If some were caught, it would only set the rest of them off laughing. The ABC was similarly easy to get into. The Classic was the hardest. A black man worked there who they called Nose, because he had the biggest, ugliest nose they had ever seen. He was not someone who could be easily fooled, and he was always quick to call the police. But that didn't deter them. One of the gang would pay to go in, another would keep Nose busy, and then the one with the ticket would go to the emergency doors and open them for the rest. Even then, they were not guaranteed to see the film, because Nose would often walk around the cinema with his flashlight, asking to see tickets and keeping his eyes open for anyone he had not seen paying to get in. Tee was usually the one who did actually pay, because Nose knew his face well. Nose didn't like him; he didn't like any of them, and they didn't like Nose.

Tee loved Pearl and her husband, Mr H, and when he was in the mood he tried to be helpful around the house. But eventually, even Pearl couldn't help realising he was up to no good. She started questioning him and shouting at him, worrying about what he was doing when he wasn't in the house and how she could control him.

Richie and Roland knew, and were forever telling him to stop running with the bad boys, but he wouldn't listen.

'Yeah, yeah, all right,' he'd say.

'You'll end up in prison,' Roland would reply.

'Nonsense, man.'

'Don't say me never warned you, Pupatee.'

'If there's any police try stop me I'll flatten their rass,' he said.

One day, Pearl went into the room Tee shared with Roland and Richie to gather up the dirty washing, and came across all Tee's new clothes in the wardrobe.

'Pupatee,' she demanded, 'what are you up to?'

'Nothing, Sis, me did lend them things off my friends.'

'Why did they lend them to you?'

'To wear, of course,' he said, smirking.

Mr H tried talking to Tee, but he was an easy-going man and had no effect. So Pearl, at her wits' end, turned to the last resort – Joe.

'Where did you get them, boy?' he demanded when he came round.

'From me friends.' Tee was giving nothing away.

Joe was mad, too, and he and Pearl agreed they would have to take the clothes to Brixton police station. He ordered Tee to accompany him. They went

94

through the door together, but when Joe got in his car Tee walked off in the other direction.

'Boy, are you going to follow me or am I going to have to follow you?' Joe yelled. Tee paid him no attention and continued on down the road. He had become used to life without Joe and his beatings, and in any case, by now he was almost as big as his brother. He wasn't going to listen to him. And if Joe took the clothes down to the police station, nothing would come of it, and Tee would stay on at Pearl's.

One Sunday morning, Pearl was making a dinner of chicken and rice and peas. There was still an hour or two to go until it would be ready, and Tee, who needed money to go to a club called St John's that night, decided to go out and see if he could find some.

He walked out into Brockwell Park and saw a group of boys about his own age, even a bit older. But they weren't tough like him and they hardly put up a protest as he went among them, demanding money. Sadly, they didn't have much more then twenty pence on them, and Tee cursed and gave up and went home to dinner. That night, his friends had to support him, buying drinks and weed so he could have a good time.

A few weeks later, he was just about to go into the Odeon picture house, which was across the road from the police station, when two police officers suddenly appeared and grabbed him. They said one of the boys he had robbed in Brockwell Park had pointed him out. Although they didn't find anything incriminating when they searched him, and Tee would say nothing, they still held him and telephoned Pearl. She was fuming when she arrived and gave him a lecture.

'I have to go home and look after my children, Pupatee,' she said. 'So if you did what they say, then tell them.'

At last it sunk in that his family weren't going to cover for him any longer. So Tee admitted the charge, thankful that he had been caught for one of his least serious offences. They couldn't do much to him for stealing twenty pence. He was bailed to appear at Camberwell court in a month or so. The gang all told him he had nothing to worry about, and it became a big joke. But the hearing was soon upon him and, to his horror, sister Pearl stood up and told them to put him in a home because she and Mr H could no longer control him. And so it was decided that Tee should be sent away to Stamford House juvenile remand centre in Shepherd's Bush.

5

Doing Time

As the van taking him to Stamford House drove through the streets of London, Tee thought dolefully about his situation. The judge hadn't given him a particular length of sentence, but had said Tee would stay in Stamford House until his behaviour merited release and a place in a suitable hostel could be found for him. Tee didn't know whether he would be spending six weeks or six months or six years there.

The other boys in the van were amazed that Tee was being sent away for such a minor offence. Although he had committed other crimes, he had not been caught for them, so he considered his punishment unjust. Now that it was actually happening to him, being sent to an institution didn't seem so cool, and as well as feeling sorry for himself, he was resentful towards Pearl. He had been thrown away like an old boot. It did not occur to him to blame himself.

They were driven through a big blue gate, which clanged shut behind them. The van doors opened and the first thing they saw was a huge man with ginger hair and breath that smelt of extra strong mints (they later realised he sucked them to cover up the smell of booze). He introduced himself as Mr G – one of the boys whispered that he thought he was Welsh – and without further ado he marched Tee and the others to their wing, where he gave them a lecture about the rules. Dormitories to be kept tidy. No talking after lights-out. No this, no that. There seemed to be about a thousand rules and Mr G warned them that if any were broken it would mean CP. Tee didn't know what CP meant, though Mr G pronounced it with a satisfaction that hinted at its unpleasantness.

Stamford House was not a borstal, but a holding place for young teenagers who had been committed by the court into various types of care and detention. The boys were allowed to wear ordinary clothes, mostly jeans, shirts and pullovers, as long as they dressed neatly. They slept in dormitories of four or five, but each had his own corner for his bed and personal belongings. The boys in each dorm would join forces to keep it spick and span as the rules required. The meals were good, particularly Friday's fish and chips, and as there were plenty of fry-ups, they never went hungry. It was a comfortable enough place, but in those first days it felt like a prison to Tee. Life was dictated by routine. Up at seven. Shower, breakfast, line-up in the yard. Then education, lunch, more education, tea and finally association in the recreation room where there were billiard and table-tennis tables, or down to the gym and the swimming-pool. Lights-out at 9.30 sharp. Tee conformed as best he could, listening, watching, trying to fit in and not get into trouble.

He quickly worked out that his problems were going to be with the other boys. Out on the streets, Tee had been one of the toughest in his neighbourhood. But here were the hard boys, from all over London. On his very first night in the canteen, just after he sat down to eat, he had a knife drawn in his face. The owner growled at Tee that he was in his seat. Tee jumped up and told him to watch it. The boy tensed and shouted, 'Come on.' Others now jumped up, some calling the boy's name, Carbury. 'You come do it now,' he shouted again, but before Tee could do anything, staff rushed in and took Carbury away to CP.

Tee was let off with a warning, but the very next day, he was confronted by another Carbury, the first Carbury's older brother. They were known by their initials, A and M. M was in Stamford House for beating up a couple of policemen.

'Hey, star, wha you in for?' he asked Tee.

'Robbery,' Tee replied.

'Wha, a old woman?'

M clearly wanted to fight, but Tee didn't take him up. He kept out of his way for the next couple of days, and by the time A came out of CP (which Tee had discovered meant Closed Prison), things had cooled down. Trouble brewed easily, but could also be quickly forgotten.

Slowly, by standing up for himself, Tee won acceptance. He joined a gang of black boys, whose members were Slim, Henry, Dexter, Gangerdeen, BufBuf, Derek, Steve and Quena, as well as the Carburys. While these boys were as tough as any of their age – thirteen to fourteen – they were still kids, and most of what they got up to was mischief, and what they considered to be fun. But the authorities took a different view.

Education occupied most of the day, but Tee did not take much notice of the teachers. When he was in class he was always skylarking about and the rest of the time he would be sneaking out to disturb the others, or to have a quick smoke. One afternoon, when the teacher had already shouted at him and several other boys who were firing folded-up bullets of paper at each other with elastic bands, Tee loosed a particularly fat bullet which caught a white boy smack in the eye.

'I warned you, Baccass,' yelled the teacher as the injured boy howled. 'Now look what you've done. You'll have to explain this to management.'

Tee was marched off to CP, where he was searched and relieved of his tobacco, matches and Rizlas. The walls of his cell were padded like sponge and it was bare except for a mattress, a table, a chair and a piss-pot. The furniture was all fixed to the floor. It was an isolation cell, a prison within a prison. On that occasion Tee only stayed overnight, but later he was to spend more time in CP and he always hated its loneliness.

Once when he was locked up on his own he asked a member of staff to help him write home to Mama and Pops and Carl. The freedom of life in Jamaica seemed a long way off now, and he told them that although he was all right, given the circumstances, he missed them and loved them and hoped they missed him too. But when Mama's reply eventually arrived, she wrote that he clearly didn't love her, because if he did he would love himself and do better in life. It was a black time.

Many of the boys went home at weekends, and one called Rodent even escaped one day by rushing out of the gates when they were opened to let in a van. But Tee had nowhere to go and he would watch the others leaving on Saturday mornings with a sinking feeling. He would almost have welcomed going to Joe's, but his brother had completely washed his hands of him. He couldn't go to Brixton, because Pearl had decided he should stay at Stamford House to learn his lesson. Certainly he was lonely and miserable for a while, but what Pearl didn't understand was that the longer he stayed there, the more he learned to be tough and criminally minded.

While Tee resented Pearl for leaving him in there, she never abandoned him completely, and continued visiting. Eventually, he persuaded her to take him out for a weekend leave. In his initial enjoyment of the delicious home cooking, surrounded by the comfort of his family, he forgave his sister. But the pleasure of being at home with Roland and Richie soon wore off, and Pearl and Mr H couldn't keep him in, so on Saturday evening he was out roaming the streets in search of his old friends. He bumped into a mate from Stamford House, and they snatched a handbag and shared the proceeds. Then they went out to have some fun. His time inside was not teaching him anything.

Eventually, after a year, Tee's stay in Stamford House came to an end. Pearl was still reluctant to take him, so a place was found for him in a hostel.

The hostel was run by Mr P, to whom Tee took an instant dislike. But among the residential staff were a younger couple named Paul and Rose, who stayed up late drinking and smoking weed. Paul even asked Tee if he could get him some weed; he would give him cash to do so.

Tee walked out of school on the first day, and after that he rarely went back. He was also supposed to help out at the hostel, but when asked he simply refused. He was nearly fifteen now and thought he had reached the age when nobody else could control his life. And in a way he was right. The staff tried a few times to bring him into line, but faced with his stubborn determination, they gave up. They had other people to attend to. Tee retreated into his 'bad bwoy' image. Stamford House had completed his education in bad bwoy ways. He was rude and acted as if he didn't have a care in the world. He gave up even attempting to talk proper English, and once more used only pure Jamaican lingo, which some of the black boys couldn't understand, let alone the English staff and kids.

On one of his first nights back inside, he headed down to his old hang-out, Shepherd's. All the Herbies were there, though by now they had changed their name to the Young Rebels. Roland was also there, disc-jockeying and dancing as usual. Looking around him, it seemed to Tee that he and his friends were no longer boys. They were growing up, making their way, trying to make it big, and from the look of everybody's pockets and clothes, Tee had a lot of catching up to do. He made a start that same Friday night.

Each morning, he would wake up, get dressed, eat his breakfast and head down towards Brixton. It was a baking hot summer. The sky was always blue and clear, and the trees were alive with birds in full song. The streets were packed. Children played on the street corners, listening out for the jingles of the ice-cream vans, spending their pennies on sweets and lollies. Everyone seemed to be enjoying that summer, but Tee was the happiest of all. He was free.

Along the Front Line, big men hung out on the street outside the gambling houses, selling weed. Their motors would be parked near by, where they could keep an eye on them. Tee enjoyed watching the cars cruising up and down the Front Line, their drivers blowing their horns, stopping to talk, waving at people they knew, and then speeding off.

Soon Tee was back to his old tricks, pickpocketing down the 'Earth', as they called the underground, or thieving from clothes shops. He would go into the chang-ing-room with various garments and come out with only

102

one in his hand. 'Nah, too small,' he would say and leave the shop, a suit and shirt hidden beneath his outer clothes. Soon he was dressed well again, in clothes from Burton or C & A. Joe's attempts to beat right and wrong into him were long forgotten. He wanted only to be seen as hard and strong and a good thief.

Although he was still only fourteen, Tee looked older; he was big and broad, and it was rare that anyone even questioned his strength. As he progressed from crime to crime without getting caught, he began to feel invincible. No one could catch him, and even if they did, he would simply fight them off.

'Yeah, man,' the other boys would say. 'Ah Tee me ah step wid. No Babylons ah go trouble we from dem sight Tee wid we.'

Some days Tee and his gang would go from station to station working the earth. If someone felt them taking his wallet they would simply carry on, saying, 'Piss off or we'll smash you in.' The victims would stand there dumbfounded with fright and shock. They even took diabolical liberties with the police. They made blatant takes directly in front of them on the platforms and there was nothing the officers could do because there were too many in the gang. If the police so much as lifted a finger against them, Tee and the rest were ready to start a war.

And then it was back to Brixton or Stockwell or Clapham. All that mattered was that they had money and that nobody got nicked. There was scarcely time to think of their victims, for before long their heads were filled with weed and drinks, and they were bragging about how successful they had been.

Shepherd's was no longer the only hang-out. There were plenty of clubs and pubs and other places to go to: St John's Church, Lansdown Hall, the Swan, Clapham

Manor baths, Mr B's. They would venture outside the area, too, travelling free on the earth in big gangs, to get to places like the Red Lion pub in Leytonstone, Bluesville at Wood Green, and the Four Aces, Flamingo, Night Angel and 20s in the West End. After a day's thieving in the West End, they would meet at a Bengal curry house to check their stolen goods or count the money they had acquired, ordering big dinners and drinks while they did so. If the pickings had been good, those who had not had a nice touch that day would get a treat. Usually they would have some cannabis, too, bought from the Front Line. They felt like characters in a gangster movie.

Life was easy, and Tee never stopped to think about the possible consequences. This was all he wanted – stickdropping, shoplifting, clubbing, partying, smoking, drugs, eating, drinking, sleeping, and then waking up and starting all over again. Mopeds were the rage but the Young Rebels didn't bother to buy them; they just borrowed one when they needed it. All you had to do was kick down hard on the pedal to jump-start it, and away you would go.

One Saturday night Tee wanted to go to a party. The hostel had a curfew, but it was never any problem getting around that. He went up to his room at the usual bedtime, but at midnight he got dressed up and climbed out through the window. He walked to a back street where he had seen a few mopeds parked in front gardens. He passed the first one as the lights were on in the house, but the second one looked safe. He wheeled it out on to the road and jump-started it but as he was on his way up the road it suddenly cut out. He got off to check it. He tried jump-starting it again. He tried push-starting it. No matter what he did it wouldn't start.

Just then a police Rover came into view with two officers inside. They slowed down and stared at him as they passed. Then Tee saw them turn round, and he flung the moped down and started running at top speed in the direction of the hostel. He was half-way up the road when they caught up with him. The policeman in the passenger seat jumped out, threw him to the ground and got him in a neck hold. Tee tried to shake him off, but he could feel his neck might snap if he struggled too hard.

'Enough?' the policeman growled.

'Yes,' Tee managed to scream.

'Good boy,' he said. His mate helped to handcuff Tee and put him in the car, and they drove him to Carter Street police station on the Walworth Road, where Tee was charged with taking and driving away, and resisting arrest. When Tee got back to the hostel he threw himself on his bed and eventually fell asleep, as sick as a half-drowned kitten. He dreaded being sent back to Stamford House.

It was several months before the case came to court, and when it did, Tee was given a one-year care order, which simply meant he would stay in the hostel for another year. He didn't give a damn.

His fifteenth birthday came and went. By now Tee had discovered interests beyond money, drugs and drink: he had fallen for a girl. Her name was Sharon and she was staying at the same hostel. She wasn't exactly a beauty, but she had a fit body and laughed a lot, and he found her incredibly sexy. She certainly gave him the come-on. He'd never done it with a girl before, but one day he went out and bought some johnnies. That night he lay in his bed dreaming of Sharon, and when the rest of the hostel was asleep, he crept into her room and slipped into bed with her. Tee put on the johnny while she giggled silently with excitement. When he climbed on top, she guided him into her and for a moment Tee felt as if he could happily have died where he lay. She was butter and Tee was hot bread. She held on to him tightly and he held on to her.

Suddenly the light snapped on.

'Who is in here?'

Sharon pushed Tee off her and pretended to be asleep. Tee looked up and saw the old night-watchwoman. 'Tee,' she squealed. 'Back to your own bedroom.'

Then Tee heard her knocking on Mr G's door.

'Mr G, I caught Tee in bed with Sharon.'

Tee never heard any more about the incident, but Mr G did start up at him about working. He was old enough now that if he wasn't going to school at least he should find a job. Falling for Sharon had made Tee feel differently about things. He was spending less time in Brixton and more around the hostel, and he decided that perhaps now was the time to go straight and see what it felt like to work and hold down a job.

Every day he went down to the job centre and phoned up about all the vacancies, using his best English. But when he turned up for interviews and they saw he was black, they would say, 'I'm sorry, the job has been taken,' or 'We'll let you know in a week or two.' For weeks Tee came back to the hostel without success.

But eventually he got a job at a meat factory in Camberwell. He set off absolutely delighted to have secured some work at last. He had been told it was near the old ABC picture house; after that, they said, anyone round there would be able to show him where to go. He carried on walking past the cinema in the direction of East Street, and on the corner of Walworth Road he stopped by two battered old iron gates. There was still a bit of paint on them, the same blue as the gates at Stamford House. A sign was hanging from one of them, and although he couldn't read too well he recognised the word 'meat'. There was a terrible smell in the air. As he walked down the path, he passed various entrances where vans were being loaded and unloaded by men in overalls. He asked one of them where to go, and as he walked away he heard the man taking off his accent to his mates.

The stench was now so overpowering that Tee vomited on his way to the supervisor's office. The supervisor, a large white man, was dressed in a double-breasted French-cut suit with flared trousers. He told Tee the job was stuffing lorry loads of scrap meat – pork, beef, lamb, goat – into a huge mincing machine. 'If you want the job, son,' he said, 'you've got it. Ten pounds a day, cash in hand.'

Tee wasn't sure he would be able to stomach it, but he wiped his mouth and decided to give it a try. The man told him he could start straight away, and he got one of the other workers to show him the ropes. They were all about his own age. There wasn't another black face in sight, but they looked friendly enough. All around him there were men coming and going, pulling or pushing barrows piled with filthy-looking meat, some of which was tinged with green.

The smell of the place was unbelievable. As the supervisor left him beside the biggest mincing machine in the place, Tee tried not to be sick again. He was terrified even to breathe, and wondered how the others managed.

The other lads gathered round Tee. 'What's the matter, mate? You don't look too happy with your new job.' When he told them it was the smell they just said, 'You get used to it.' Then they went back to their machines and started laughing and joking again as they got on with their work. Tee couldn't join in; he was afraid to open his mouth too wide in case the foul air filled his lungs.

'You just stuff all the scrap meat in this big hole,' said Ginge, who was showing him what to do. 'When the box under the mincer is full you move it over there, and start on the next one.' Then he left him to it. Some of the meat had obviously been sitting there for weeks and was half rotten. Tee started picking up great lumps of it and stuffing it in the hole, where the blades were going round and round. It reminded him of one of those comic-book spaceships. He pushed the meat in one end, and it came out in red and brown and green twists at the other. Gradually Tee's stomach began to settle down. For some reason he hadn't been given any gloves and he worked as fast as he could to keep his mind off the feeling of the rancid flesh on his bare hands. It was only when the machine started making a strange whining noise that he saw it had stopped spinning and was completely clogged up with meat.

'Turn it off!' he heard someone shout. 'The red button at the side!'

Ginge came over. 'Try not to put too much in at once, mate, or you'll spend the whole day clearing out the mincer instead of working it.'

Tee thanked him.

'No problem,' he said. 'Just give me a shout if you're not sure about anything.'

One of the other lads was a Hell's Angel, and he seemed to fool around all day. He claimed that he stuffed his machine with anything he could find – dead rats, blackbirds, baby mice. 'Throw it all fucking in, mate,' he said. 'Who gives a fuck anyway? All you do is make sure you don't eat no mince from round here.'

Somehow Tee made it to the end of the day. But that night, on the way home, people held their noses on the bus. He was so embarrassed that he got off and walked the rest of the way. When he got back to the hostel, Sharon wouldn't go near him. He had four baths before he could get the stink off him, and threw the jacket, jeans and monkey boots he had been wearing into the bin. The next morning, when the staff woke him up for work, he told them the only way they would get him back to the factory was as dead meat himself.

Tee soon found another job, this time in a carpentry workshop. It was easier work and the only smell was of wood shavings, but sliding planks through a rotary saw all day was very boring. It was not long before he became restless. Working life didn't compare to a life of crime. There were no thrills to be had, and it certainly didn't pay so well. Tee started on a Monday, and by Wednesday his attention had turned to a full-length, brand-new sheepskin coat hanging on the rack. Just before dinner he took it and left, and headed to Brixton, dressed in his new finery. The coat was much admired, and eventually Tee swapped it for a leather suit and twenty pounds in cash.

He was right back into his bad ways. Every morning he would make straight for Brixton and join up with all his friends. His gang began to have run-ins with the Old Bill, but there were usually just a couple of policemen and half a dozen big Brixton boys. If the pigs grabbed anyone, the others would rush to help, with Tee usually at the lead. When Tee heard a policeman refer to him as 'that big black police GBH-er', it only boosted his ego further. He thought he was the up-and-coming notorious 'bad bwoy' and he loved it when friends patted his back and shook his hand. Everywhere he went he got respect. He was seeing less of Sharon, but now that he was back out on the streets and making a success of it, other girls were starting to show an interest.

One afternoon, down the earth, Tee took a wallet from a tourist's handbag and found it contained £1,800 – the most money he had ever seen. For weeks he was splashing cash all over the place, treating friends and buying things for girls, and the next time a party was heading for the earth, he still had £500 left. Everyone else was stickdropping like crazy but Tee was just watching, his pockets already full. Suddenly, four uniformed policemen showed up and went straight for him. There was a big fight, but eventually they overpowered him and took him to West End Central police station, where they gave him a good hiding.

They asked who all the other kids were, but Tee told them he didn't know. Then they locked him up.

A little later, a big plain-clothes policeman came into the cell. He looked rough and mean, like the Devil himself. He walked over to Tee, grinding his teeth, his face all vexed up. Two others came in behind him and locked the door. Tee stood up and stared at this man, wondering what he had got himself into. Suddenly Tee was really frightened.

Without warning, the copper grabbed him, almost lifting him off the ground. 'You see this, sonny Jim?' he said, showing his clenched fist. It was like a sledge-hammer that had seen better days; Tee couldn't see the knuckles for all the lumps and scars. 'I did this on a black man's head. Unless you want me to do it all over your little black face you'd better give me the names and addresses of some of them boys who were pickpocketing with you today in the underground. All right?'

'I don't know them,' Tee insisted.

'Listen!' he growled, 'I won't tell you again what I'll do to you.' And he pushed his fist into Tee's face.

'I don't know them,' Tee said again.

'Names,' he said, forcing his fist harder into Tee's face, almost blocking out the light. 'Names and addresses.'

Tee was frightened now and he began to whimper. He wasn't so tough any more. Then the other two men moved in.

'Come on, Harry, that will do,' said one of them.

'But I'll make him talk.'

'Nah, we'll just charge him.'

They had found about four empty purses in the station, and after charging Tee with theft, two assaults, resisting arrest and attempted theft, they let him out on police bail.

When he reappeared in Brixton a couple of days later, he was given a hero's welcome for not grassing anyone up, and he was showered with money, weed and drinks. Within a few days he had forgotten how scared he'd been at the police station and was at it again, but determined not to get nicked this time. He bought a big lock knife, and carried it everywhere.

Some time later, dropping sticks down at Victoria station, Tee noticed one of his pals being arrested. He ran over and pulled out his knife. The policemen backed away and Tee and his friends jumped on a train, but just as it was pulling away another copper appeared. He was one of the policemen from West End Central who had arrested Tee, and he called out his name. But the doors closed, Tee gave him two fingers, and in a moment the train was pulling away down the tunnel.

That night, they all ended up at the Sundown across

111

the road from Brixton police station. Tee was having a really good time, drinking, smoking, laughing and dancing with all his friends. When the club closed, like a fool Tee went back to the hostel and climbed into bed with Sharon. A couple of hours later they woke up to find the room filled with police officers. Tee was handcuffed and taken down to West End Central where he was locked up. The next day they took him to court for all the pickpocket charges, the knife, assault and more, and this time Tee was remanded in custody.

He was kept on remand for two months. He hated every second. The staff were bullies and he was locked up for hours at a time. The food was awful, he had nothing to smoke and nothing to occupy him, and not a single friend. Nobody visited him except Pearl. Time dragged by.

Eventually Tee was found guilty on all counts and taken to the Inner London Crown court for sentencing. He looked around the courtroom but his friends had all abandoned him. The only person he knew was Pearl.

'Madam,' the judge asked her, 'do you have anything to say on behalf of your brother before I pass sentence?'

'Yes, your Honour. I beg you, please, not to send him to prison but to deport him to his mother and father in Jamaica.'

'Thank you,' said the judge. 'Baccass, stand up! You are here to be sentenced for a number of very serious offences ranging from pickpocketing to assault to offences with a knife, as well as many lesser crimes, which have been taken into consideration. But before I pass sentence I must ask you whether you would like to return to your mother and father in Jamaica. You do realise that if you stay in this country you will have to behave yourself.'

'Yes, your Honour.'

112

'So, which is it? Staying here or returning to Jamaica?'

The judge had spoken so kindly and his words about behaving himself persuaded Tee that he was going to be given a chance and set free. Although a part of him yearned for Jamaica, it was like a dream, for he barely remembered it. Brixton was his life now. 'I'll stay here, your Honour,' he said.

Tee heard Pearl sigh sadly.

'So be it, Baccass,' the judge said. 'I am going to give you the chance to settle down and become a good boy by giving you two years of borstal training.'

When Tee reached Wormwood Scrubs that night he wanted to cry for Mama and Pops, for the chance he had missed. But he couldn't cry; he was too frightened. Everything he cared about was lost – the friends he had grown up with, the girl he loved, Richie and Roland, the clubs and parties and fine clothes. He had lost the world, and the world had lost him. All he had now was this big dirty jail with its never-ending iron bars and locked doors and the smell of Old Holborn tobacco everywhere. It was different from Stamford House. The officers reminded him of German soldiers in prisoner-of-war films, with their big bunches of keys, shouting at the inmates, 'Tuck your shirt in, boy,' or 'Button up your jacket,' or 'Get your hand out of your pocket,' or 'No talking,' or 'You have been placed on report.' There was no freedom of any sort. He had thought his life with Joe was tough, but now he realised how hard things could really be.

He was put on the borstal allocation wing, along with all the other boys waiting to be sent off to Feltham or Huntercombe or Finnemore Wood.

Sister Pearl and Roland visited him, as did sister

113

Ivy. But his friends never came, and he sat in his cell both missing them and hating them for leading him into a life of crime. He never once thought to blame himself. All he wanted was to be back out there, clubbing and smoking a joint. But where the body cannot go, the mind can, and he spent hours dreaming of the streets; if he heard there was a party or a particular club going on, he would imagine himself there with his friends, smoking, drinking, dancing and romancing.

That way he survived, and slowly he began to accept his situation, and to laugh and play and joke like the other borstal boys. He signed up for education to help him learn to write, and joined in with sports down at the gym. And so the days turned into weeks and the weeks into months.

At night, there would be shouting out of the windows between the borstal boys and the older convicts.

'Hey, cons,' one of the borstal boys would shout, 'who's giving your missus one tonight, then?'

'Someone with a bit more fucking sense than you, borstal boy,' would come the reply.

The same shouting went back and forth for half the night.

Tee's efforts to read and write frustrated him so much that he ended up shouting at the teachers and being kicked out of education. He was now down in the workshops, and it wasn't long before he was getting into trouble there. One afternoon, when he was dying for a smoke, he saw a white boy take out his full baccy tin and make a nice fat roll-up. By this time Tee's mouth was watering and he went over and said, 'Spare us one till I get my pay, mate.'

'No.'

Tee got mad and snatched the roll-up out of the boy's

mouth. The boy grabbed Tee with both hands on his collar.

'Give it back!' he shouted.

'Let go!'

'Give it back!'

Tee saw red and pulled his head back to give the boy an almighty head-butt that broke his nose, flattening it against his face. But he was a tough Northerner, and he kept his grip on Tee. They fell together to the floor, wrestling each other. Tee managed to get on top and he pulled back his clenched fist to hammer the boy's head off with every bit of his strength, but his opponent saw it coming; he jerked his head sideways and Tee's fist hit the floor with an almighty smack.

The floor was made of solid concrete, and Tee felt his fist disintegrate. He tried to scream with pain, but nothing came out. The workshop officer had seen them now, and he pressed the alarm and pulled them apart. Officers ran through the corridors and dragged both of them to the block.

The next day they told the governor they hadn't been fighting, just messing about, and they were let off with a caution. On their way back to the wing, they smiled and shook hands. The boy mentioned something about his nose, which was all over his face, and Tee showed him his fist, with all the knuckles raw where the skin had been shredded by the workshop floor. They ended up at the sickbay together. The boy's name was McNelly, and soon Tee and he were good friends. It was like Brixton, like boys in many places: first the fight, then the friendship.

Finally, the day came for Tee's allocation. He was given Feltham, known as Feltham Nut-house, the worst of all the borstals. He rode down there in a van with several other boys. It wasn't a long journey from

115

the Scrubs, and it was hard to see anything from the tiny window of the van. It felt odd travelling like that, sealed off from the world, but that was his life now.

The van turned in through the gates of Feltham and the boys were dropped off at Centre House for induction. All new receptions spent a week here, before being assigned to one of the house blocks – North, South, East, West or the residential part of Centre itself. That week they were shown around and instructed on how to behave while at the borstal. Tee could have counted the number of other black boys on one hand, and half of them seemed to be already gone in the head. He soon understood that North House was mainly for boys with a history of drug abuse, East House was for violent boys, South House for sex offenders and West House for the saps who couldn't fight their way out of a wet paper bag. Apart from the receptions, Centre House was for boys who had many, or all, of these faults.

When the time came for house allocation, Tee was taken into an office with three members of staff – a fat man with a red face who looked friendly enough but didn't say much, a big thug, and a mean-looking, rat-like one who did all the talking. He was asked if he took drugs, whether he was gay, whether he liked to fight, and many other questions. He replied no to almost everything, and was put in East House, allocated to a dormitory with fourteen others. The East House lads were the toughest at Feltham, but he wasn't going to be afraid of that.

What frightened him more was South House, which was separated from East only by a big gate with bars, through which the two lots of boys could see each other. Tee couldn't believe his eyes. A number of the South House lot were dressed up like girls, wearing

116

lipstick and make-up. If you hadn't known they were boys you could have been fooled into thinking they were sexy, the way they walked around, wriggling their waists and backsides. Some of them were as dashing as any girl out on the street. They even talked in high voices and laughed like women. They were called queens, and each queen had a rougher-looking partner. These were the butches.

The boys from East Wing would call the queens by their female nicknames, shouting over to them things like, 'Show us your tits, Sally.' The reply would be, 'You're not going to see anything, but I'll show that hunk of a black man who just came in. He's gorgeous, hasn't he got strong muscles? I'll bet he's got a big one.' To Tee's surprise, they were talking about him and it was only his dark complexion that hid his embarrassment.

On Tee's first day, one of the toughest lads, called Hunter, sent a messenger to ask him for twenty pence protection money. The first time, Tee told the messenger he should be giving Tee money to protect him. The second time Tee pulled him up and growled at him that if he asked him a third time he would rip his head off his shoulders. 'It's not me, mate,' the boy protested. 'I'm only doing what I've been told, like.' He walked off with a shrug, as if to say he had been warned, that Hunter was not to be messed with.

Quite a lot of the boys, Tee included, were on medication to control their behaviour. They had to go down to the sickbay twice a day to take a liquid cosh which would make them less violent, but Tee learned to keep it in his mouth without swallowing, and spit it out as soon as he could. It took a while to get used to the horrible taste, so for the first few days he would go straight to the bathroom to clean his teeth. On his way

117

to get his toothbrush out of the locker, Tee would pass the big hall where they all ate and watched television. It was a big, echoing place, with three rows of chairs and tables set out in straight lines. The bathroom was the same. The first things you would see were a row of basins and a row of toilets, and if you turned left from there you came down a passage to the showers and baths, which were also in lines. At the end of the baths was an empty room which they said was supposed to be turned into a sauna, but it was used by the boys as a place to sort out fights.

That first evening, Tee stored his toothbrush in his locker again and put the key in his pocket. The key was tied to a shoelace, which was attached to the belt loop above his pocket. After tea there was a film on television and he sat in the front row, so caught up by the action on the screen that he didn't notice his key being lifted. It was only after the film when he went to get something from his locker that he realised his key had gone. He instantly started shouting that whoever had taken it was going to get knocked out. Most of the boys ignored him, but a group of them stood there laughing, including Hunter, the boy who ran the protection racket.

Everyone was dispersing now to get things done before bedtime, some to see their friends in the record room, others to visit the matron. Tee searched around for suspects. The hall was closing down for the evening; the tables were all packed on top of each other, and the chairs in stacks. Boys were starting to head up to their sleeping quarters. They all avoided Tee, until a boy named Al passed him and said, 'Hunter has your key, but don't tell him I told you'.

Tee found Hunter and demanded his key. Hunter was a thin, wiry boy with mean blue eyes.

'What?' said Hunter. 'Go away, you're not worth it.'

Tee moved closer to him, clenching his fists.

'OK try it then,' he said. 'You want to fight, do you? I told you you weren't worth it.'

Without warning Hunter threw a right to Tee's face, catching him off guard, and landing him on his arse. Tee jumped up and was just steaming in with kicks and a punch when Mr J, the assistant wing governor, came in. 'Stop it!' he shouted. 'Any more from you two and you'll both be down the block.' When they had separated, he asked what it was all about.

Fuming, Tee said he just wanted his locker key.

'Hunter, have you got his key?' Mr J asked, folding his arms impatiently.

The boy said nothing, but took the key out of his pocket and handed it to Tee. Mr J let them off with a warning. Tee went straight to his locker to make sure nothing had been nicked, and when he opened it he was greeted by the awful smell of shit. There was a cup of it in his locker, and a note saying, 'Your family and you are made from this crap.'

To add to Tee's fury, there wasn't anything he could do right now. He had to sweep up the dining-hall as punishment for being the last into bed on previous nights, and Mr J was waiting for him. Everyone else had gone. Tee fetched the broom from the cupboard under the stairs and was about to start sweeping when he heard a shout above him. He looked up and saw Hunter, split seconds before a blob of spit caught him flush in the face. Suddenly something snapped in him. He broke the broomstick against a post and charged up the stairs after Hunter's blood. Half-way up he met Hunter and his gang coming down to meet him. He laid into them with the broken end of the broomstick, clubbing and swinging and stabbing. But there were too many of them, and they managed to get it off him. They all came at him at once. He ran back down and jumped over a table, intending to keep the gang off by firing punches at them from behind it, but Mr J and two other members of staff arrived to break up the fight.

This time Hunter and Tee were taken down to the block. To Tee's satisfaction, he had managed to rearrange Hunter's face; his enemy's eyes, nose, lips and cheeks were all bleeding. A couple of days later they were brought in front of the governor. Hunter was given another month on his sentence, but Tee got two months, because Hunter and the other boys were hurt, while he hadn't sustained a single bruise.

The governor also ordered that Tee be kept down in the block and it was another five weeks before the borstal doctor, a woman named Dr More, came to see him and recommended that he go back to the house again. As he walked down the passage where the assistant governor and matron had their offices, he saw the whole house at the end. They started running towards him and he thought: Oh no, not again. But when they got to him they lifted him up, laughing and joking, and welcoming him back.

Even Hunter seemed glad to see him back from the block, telling him he was the chap now and giving him burn and a couple of spliffs. Tee felt like a hero.

Tee was now in a single cell because the staff didn't trust him to share. But the lads were all nice to him, and he got plenty of smoke and hash and money.

Everyone had to go to work or training, and there were courses in painting and decorating, concrete moulding and bricklaying, as well as jobs in the kitchen, works, gardens and so on. Each morning they would leave the wings and line up in the yard until their names were called to join the work party. Tee chose bricklaying. He tried to improve his English so that he could be understood better. He was fed up with being laughed at because of his accent. Proper English was like another language to him. As he began to master it the boys mocked him less and soon he found he had two languages: his own and English. He began to settle down. But he had not forgotten those boys who had tried to hurt him. Their faces were a permanent picture in his mind. Deep inside, it was far from laid to rest, but now he was playing wise to catch wise.

One day, after dinner, he called Hunter and they went round the back of the shower. 'Hunter, you might have forgotten, but I have not forgotten,' he said. Then – smack! – he chinned Hunter and dropped him to the ground. 'Get up,' he ordered him, and then landed a kick in Hunter's chest that winded him for a minute. When Hunter could breathe again he begged Tee not to carry on. Tee felt great Hunter was frightened and wouldn't even fight back. Tee pulled him to his feet and shook his hand, telling him never to cross him again.

From that day on, Hunter was his biggest joke. A couple of days later, Tee pulled another of the gang, Nicky, who counted himself a Hell's Angel. At the first punch to his chest, Nicky doubled up on the ground, and Tee kicked him a few times. He proved to be nothing on his own, and it was the same with Jeff. The rest of the gang had been discharged, but Tee had revenged himself.

A few months later, a boy called Bob returned to Feltham. He had been in Hunter's initial gang but left before Tee got out of the block. He had heard about his three mates being beaten up, and set about trying to be closer than a brother to Tee, laughing and joking and giving him roll-ups. But Tee remembered the night when Bob had ganged up against him in the fight.

'Guess what, Bob,' he said one day. It was the weekend and most of the others had gone to the borstal club, leaving them almost alone on the wing.

'What?'

'There is going to be a fight today. A big fight.'

'Who? Tee, let me beat him up for you.'

'Let's go round the back of the shower where we can talk.' Bob followed Tee keenly, wanting to know who he was going to fight.

'Who, Tee? Let me knock him out, whoever he is.'

'You don't understand Bob,' he said. 'You are going to need all your strength for yourself, cause it's me and you who is going to fight.'

Bob suddenly went grey, saying, 'Leave it out, Tee, we're mates.' He slapped Tee in a friendly way, trying to joke it off.

'Take your hands off me, Bob,' said Tee. Bob looked worried and confused and frightened. 'I'll never forget how you tried hard to bash me and the rage in your face and your eyes. So I'm just going to give you the chance to fulfil your dream now, that's all.'

'Come on, Tee, that was a year ago.'

'Maybe so, but I haven't forgotten. So let's cut the talk and fight.' Tee stood in front of him and said, 'Throw your blow.' Bob didn't want to but eventually he said, 'Well, if that's what you want.' He shook his shoulders and fired a left at Tee's face. It rocked Tee, but in reply Tee let out a string of lefts and rights into Bob's face and solar plexus, downing him.

'Get up, you lazy git,' he said, kicking him. Bob tugged at his foot and said, 'Come on, Tee, let's call it a day.'

Reluctantly Tee backed off. Both Bob's eyes were swollen; his lips were fat and his nose was bleeding.

Tee felt his own lips. They were fat too. They cleaned themselves up and went back into the dining-hall, laughing and talking. They passed one of the officers who asked what had happened to their faces.

'I knocked my face on the wall, guv,' said Tee.

'I slipped on a bar of soap in the shower,' added Bob.

'You expect me to believe that load of cock and bull?'

'It's the truth, guv.'

The officer looked at them and said, 'Go on, get out of my sight before I place the pair of you under investigation. You must think I was born yesterday.'

Tee's vendetta was over, but not the fighting. He would beat up anyone to take their money and their burn, but the more restless and bored he became, the more he took to bullying other boys simply for something to do. There was little else for entertainment, and in any case, Tee had got a taste for it. He enjoyed being top of the heap, and he enjoyed bending others to his will.

On the occasions when his family came to see him Tee would not be such a tough guy. When he was first inside he sent out Visiting Orders as often as he was allowed. Pearl would come, or sister Ivy, and they would bring delicious home-cooked meals with them – rice and peas and chicken, or fried fish with hard dough bread, which he adored. Although he wasn't supposed to eat this food, the officers always turned a blind eye while he gobbled it up. But it was hard seeing people from outside. They didn't have much to say to him, and sat there looking as if they wanted to leave again. Tee was ashamed of his surroundings. He tried to joke with Roland about what was going on down the clubs, but hearing about it made him feel worse about what he was missing. Most of all, he found it hard seeing the hurt in sister Pearl's eyes. After a while he stopped sending out VOs.

Eventually, after nineteen months had passed, Tee was given his first home leave. It was wonderful walking down the street to Feltham railway station to catch the train. Tee was full of excitement about seeing his family and friends and Brixton again. He got off the train at Clapham Junction and as he walked up the street to the bus-stop, he passed some men's clothes shops. They had some beautiful menswear in them, but he overcame the temptation to go back to his old ways, and walked on.

When he reached the bus-stop, who should he see waiting there but sister Pearl herself. They were delighted to see each other and hugged and kissed. They travelled to Kellett Road together and joined up with Roland, Richie, Selena and Mr H. The house felt so comfortable and familiar, and the air was filled with the mouth-watering smell of Jamaican pepper-pot stew which had been simmering all day in his honour. The whole family gathered around the table to have supper together, and Tee felt happier than he could remember.

It was a Friday night, and when Tee had eaten he couldn't wait to go out and see his friends. It felt so good to be free of rules and to be able to do exactly what he wanted. He and Roland headed straight for Shepherd's. Although his friends hadn't seen Tee for well over a year, none of them seemed surprised to see him walk in, and they gave him a hero's welcome. He remembered how nobody had come to visit him inside, but they all slapped him on the back, and gave him weed, and bought him drinks, and soon any resentment he had stored up was forgotten. He was enjoying the smoky atmosphere, trading jokes with his friends and eyeing up the girls just as he always had. It didn't matter that he had no money, because his friends paid for everything he needed that weekend. All in all, he had a great time. He felt like somebody again.

It was grim going back to borstal on Sunday evening, but Tee had an ounce of strong black Stevetmas hash in his pocket given to him by Big Youth, which made him feel better. On the way in, he hid it by one of the lights and collected it the next evening. Then he transferred it to a book he had hollowed out in his cell, to keep for Christmas which was only twelve days away. Now he had something to look forward to.

The next day, he was brewing up tea when an officer came for him to say he was wanted on the house block. When Tee got there he was told his cell was going to be searched. Did he have anything he wanted to tell them about? 'No,' he said. Two officers searched the whole cell, all except the book shelf. 'That's it,' one of them announced. But just as they were about to leave, the other said, 'We haven't checked the books, have we?'

He went over to the book shelf, opened up the book and found Tee's ounce of black hash. Tee was devastated. Not only had he lost his Christmas treat, but now he had to worry about what would happen to his discharge date. Smuggling drugs inside was a serious offence.

He was taken down to the block and the police were called, and though Tee wasn't charged he lost another three months.

He was soon back to his old ways, fighting and abusing the officers and getting nicked and being put under investigation. He seemed to get in trouble almost every day. His weekend out was a dim memory, except for the trouble it had landed him in, and he no longer cared about anything. Gradually the weeks slid into months.

Then, one morning, two officers came to his cell and said, 'Up you get, Tee, and pack your kit.' This was what they always said when he was under investigation or being placed on report.

'What have I done now, guv?' he asked.

'Just pack your kit and follow us,' was the reply.

They led him straight towards the block. When he got there he dropped his kit, waiting for them to open it up. But they kept on walking and did not stop until they reached the discharge room.

'We are giving you a discharge,' they said when he had caught up. 'Think yourself lucky we don't take you back to court and let you start a fresh whack of borstal, because as far as we're concerned you have learned nothing on this sentence. You've got half an hour to get out of the borstal grounds or we'll call the police and have you arrested.'

Tee didn't need half an hour. Within half a minute he was hurrying down the road to the station.

Tee soon learned that things in Brixton had moved on. Stickdropping and shoplifting were still popular, but quite a few of the lads were now into robbery and putting women on the game. Some had taken to kiting – cheque-book and cheque-card fraud – and others burglary.

But Tee had a bit of cash to keep him going. While he was inside, the Criminal Compensation Board had paid out for his injuries at the fair, and sister Pearl had put the money, £128, into a post office savings account in his name. Before he started trying to get any more, he had other things to do.

Tee was sixteen, and he had hardly seen a woman since he was sent away. Sharon, the only girl he'd ever been with, was long gone. He might have been experienced with crime and police stations and prison, but he was still quite new to the world of women. So when he bumped into Girlie a day or two after coming out, he was ready for anything.

Girlie was a half-caste girl from Peckham whom he had known since his childhood. She was pretty, with a big Afro hairstyle like the Jackson Brothers, and she spoke pure cockney. When they met she was dressed in her school uniform of white socks, blue skirt and white shirt. Girlie promised to meet him at Shepherd's on his first Friday night out, and the three days until then seemed as long as all the time he had spent in borstal. When the night finally arrived, he asked her if she would go out with him.

'All right,' she said.

He couldn't believe his ears. He was so happy. This was going to be the start of something new.

They decided to go on to a club called the Four Aces in north London. After stopping at the Clapham Wimpy House, they went north over the river. Girlie held his arm as they entered the club and Tee felt as proud as anything. He finally had a girlfriend as beautiful as any girl in London.

The music was kicking up like an excited donkey and Tee bought them drinks at the bar. Girlie started dancing in front of him, and soon he was dancing with her. After a while, Tee reached out and touched her and she came into his arms and he held her tight.

Later that night they danced the rubberdub, which was as close as you could get to making love without going to bed, and then they talked and laughed, as if they belonged to each other. It wasn't until the early hours of the morning that they left to make their way back over the river.

Tee had fallen in love with Girlie. She had been

127

around while he was growing up and had always been sweet. But now, on top of that she had grown into a woman with everything a man could wish for. Over the weeks that followed they grew closer and closer. Tee had never been happier.

Tee's love life might be going smoothly, but in other ways the officers at Feltham were proved right – he was as far from learning his lesson as he had ever been.

When he ran out of money he joined up again with the stickdroppers. It didn't matter whether he was on his own or with other people, he went wild at it. Once he was seen by a policeman, but he managed to beat him up and get away. Fortunately, it was not a policeman who knew Tee. But then came the day when he was arrested again for pickpocketing. This time his violent attempts to escape were not successful and he was remanded on the usual string of charges of theft, assault and possession of an offensive weapon – a new knife he had taken to carrying wherever he went. So there he was, only months since he had left Feltham, back inside, with only the compensation of being visited by Girlie. She was doing all right. She had left school now and was working as a telephonist.

From remand, Tee went to the Scrubs, then Feltham again, and then on to Finnemore Wood. It wasn't easy for Girlie to get to see him there but she came when she could, and although he was only in for six months this time, it was long enough for him to realise how much he loved Girlie and wanted to be with her. She was the first person he went to see on his release, and she greeted him with delight. This time, he told her, he was determined to go straight, to make her proud of him. He was living with sister Ivy now, and he got a job

128

with the council as a gardener, working in Stockwell Park. It wasn't much, but it was a start. His friends would come by, trying to persuade him to give it up and go stickdropping with them, showing him the wads of money they had in their pockets. Helped by Girlie, Tee ignored them and kept working hard. But then one day the council discovered he had a criminal record, which he had not told them, and he got the sack. He tried for a bit to get another job, but nobody was interested in him, so he was soon back to his life of crime.

This time he had a longer run before he had any trouble with the police, but eventually the inevitable happened and he was picked up. He got bail, and when he saw Girlie she was furious with him. He didn't like to make her unhappy, but he was getting used to doing what he wanted – sister Ivy was no better at controlling him than Pearl had been – and he resented being told how to behave. Girlie backed off and he carried on with his way of life regardless, heading helter-skelter to his next meeting with the law.

It came when he was stickdropping from bus-stop to bus-stop in Clapham Common. Two plain-clothes policemen tried to grab him and a big fight ensued. They were no match for Tee. A black bus inspector even came to their aid, but he ended up getting beaten along with them. Tee made his escape down Crescent Lane and hid up in Grovesnor House flats, but they came after him, carrying out a door-to-door search until they found Tee and dragged him down to Clapham station.

The coppers at the station made it clear that they were going to give Tee a good hiding, but he was saved by the arresting officer who said, 'It's all right, lads, he's going to give us a long statement.' Then he turned to Tee. 'Aren't you? Say yes, for fuck's sake.' Tee realised he had better do as he was told, so he agreed.

'What?' one of the other policemen shouted. 'I can't hear you.'

'I'm going to write a long statement,' Tee repeated.

'What?' they all screamed, their hands at their ears.

He shouted his reply this time, so that they could hear it loud and clear. They all looked disappointed. He signed the statement without bothering to find out what was in it. He was beyond caring and they had so much on him anyway that it didn't matter what was written down. The only thing that interested him was the parcel of fish and chips which sister Ivy sent when she was informed of his whereabouts.

He was taken to South-western magistrates' court in Lavender Hill where the magistrate said bail was out of the question – he was sending the case to the Inner London Crown court, recommending that Tee go to prison for a long, long time. Then he was taken off to Wormwood Scrubs on remand. The procedure was becoming routine to him. When the case came up at the ILCC, Tee pleaded guilty. The judge stared down at him and gave him a lecture about his crimes.

Then he said he was giving Tee a sentence of eighteen months, suspended for two years. Tee was amazed and delighted. He had been given one last chance.

But even so, and even with Girlie's love, he still could not stay out of trouble. He liked taking her out at the weekends and showing her off, but her telephonist job kept her busy during the day, and often when she finished she was too tired to go out clubbing. Staying in and watching television didn't interest him – he'd had enough of that in the nick – so he was soon meeting up with his old friends, Rodent, D, Staff, Igus, Boobs, Big Youth, Mike, Jack Ranking, Natty Dennis, Dirty H,

Chipper and Buzzer. Some had jobs, but it was difficult even for those who did. While Tee was inside the notorious Sus laws had been passed, and even innocent black boys in Brixton were being stopped simply for walking down the street. There were boys Tee knew who wanted to go straight, or were going straight, or had never been anything other than straight, but who were stopped so many times on Sus that they gave up and started doing what the police assumed they had been up to in the first place. But most of Tee's friends were into crime anyway, and even though Girlie pleaded with him to live an honest life, he was soon back at picking pockets.

This time he had a good run of about six months without any trouble from the Old Bill. Then one day he was with some lads down the earth, doing the Piccadilly line. They were now rougher and braver than they had ever been and some of the time they scarcely bothered to pick pockets – they just robbed passengers at will, taking their wallets and bags in front of their eyes. The train they were on pulled out from Russell Square, heading north, but it stopped as soon as it entered the tunnel, and stayed there for several minutes. Someone must have raised the alarm, because when the train finally pulled into the next station, King's Cross, uniformed police officers were waiting. They came on board and as they started searching people, one of them practically pounced on Tee.

'I know this one,' he said.

'Leave him,' the sergeant replied.

'But it's Tee, the police GBHer,' the other shouted out.

'All right, keep an eye on him.'

Pretty soon Tee and his friends had been arrested for

conspiracy and attempted theft. After some weeks on remand, although the lads who had been with him when he was arrested got off, Tee was found guilty and given twenty-one months at Aylesbury Young Offenders Institution.

Aylesbury was a step up from Feltham, much tougher and tenser. The regime was hard, but as at borstal, the other inmates presented more of a worry than the screws. The boys here were only a step down from full-grown men and they carried themselves as such. Here were some of the toughest young criminals in England. Some of them Tee already knew from Stamford House, like the Carbury brothers and Steve – who were part of the Deptford Axe gang which had gone on a rampage of armed robberies – others like Mastive, Patrick, Jimmy and Fingers were Brixtonites. There were hard nuts from Birmingham and places further north, and muggers, burglars and even killers.

His first few days, Tee felt very small and sad, and he kept to himself and busied himself in the laundry house where he was put to work. The cells at Aylesbury were real cells, with bars on the windows like in an adult prison. In that hot summer, it was like an oven in there. But Tee's reputation preceded him, and it did not take him long to start to live up to it and to find his place among the toughest of the Aylesbury inmates.

In the laundry, Tee soon took the best position, which involved searching pockets before clothes went into the wash. Anything like money or tobacco that had been carelessly left in a pocket became Tee's.

His anger and frustration still sometimes got the better of him. Although he was seldom challenged by the other boys he did occasionally get into fights, and ended up down in the block. But as the weeks went by, Tee adapted to life in Aylesbury as he had at Stamford House and Feltham, and soon the weeks grew into months and the months into a year. And eventually, his sentence came to an end, and it was time for Tee to rejoin the world, to return to Brixton and Girlie and whatever life had in store for him.

6

Girlie

The first thing Tee did when he returned to London was go to a sauna and steam the grime and smell and memories of the prison out of his pores. Then he went to find Girlie, who was there waiting for him, beautiful as ever. He felt like a man, twenty feet tall, having a stunner like her.

His room at Kellett Road was waiting for him, too. He was welcomed home and heard all the news. Roland was still writing songs, singing and dancing, playing the superstar he wanted to become. Richie and Selena were both growing up. Pearl's cooking was as delicious as ever, and she and Mr H even agreed to Girlie moving in as well. They thought she might steady him.

Girlie was working hard. She had never committed a single crime in her whole young life. Tee knew that he loved her, and had decided in prison that he wanted to have a baby with her. She thought it was a good idea too, but it meant he would have to go straight, so for a few weeks he looked for a job. But when he didn't find one, it was as if something inside him simply shrugged away memories of prison and fears of returning in the future. He didn't know what to do with his blotted life, and once again it was not long before he was drifting back in the wrong direction, towards trouble.

All around him, the people he knew were involved in criminal activities. The big men were selling weed and hash, running gambling houses, keeping clubs. Some were into armed robberies. Others were notorious pimps and ponces.

At weekends, Girlie and Tee were always together, but during the week when she was off at work he started picking pockets again, working bus-stops, pubs and anywhere else there were crowds of people, like Madame Tussaud's or Victoria coach station. He was nineteen years old now, still young, but big and tough.

Tee used the money he stole to buy himself smart new outfits, and with these he was ready for a new crime he had learned about in prison, called creeping.

One day, he went out dressed in a white shirt, black tie and black wool suit, with a reversible raincoat thrown over his arm. He looked like any other hard-working office employee, or at least that was what he hoped.

He walked past a big office building, checking to see who was on the front desk, then did a U-turn and entered, behaving as if he was looking for somebody. When no one noticed him for what he really was, he took a lift up to one of the floors and walked about confidently, making out that he had as much right to be in the office as anyone. He had picked a good time, dinner hour, when people were relaxing or were out of the office. He knocked on several doors. When someone said 'Come in,' he would ask for Mr Taylor or Mrs Galloway or Miss Collins, and when he was told they did not work there, he thanked them and left. These offices did not interest him. It was the ones where he got no answer that were Tee's aim. When he knocked and heard nothing he opened the door and crept in.

In one of these empty offices he found a woman's handbag, and when he opened it his heart skipped a beat. Inside the bag was nestled a large pay packet. Tee snatched it out, along with a purse and some gold jewellery. There was time to search for more, but he knew he had a touch, so he turned to leave. As he opened the door, he saw a man and a woman sitting at their desks. His mind racing, Tee crept silently out. Instead of walking normally, he went slowly backwards, so when some change tinkled in his pocket and the people turned round, it looked as if he was just walking into the offices.

'Can we help you, sir?' the woman asked.

Tee smiled to himself because his trick had worked. 'I'm looking for a job as an office cleaner,' he said in his best voice.

'Sorry, we have our own office cleaners. There are no jobs here, I'm afraid.'

'Thank you anyway, madam.' Tee smiled and left. Outside, he hailed a taxi and told the driver to take him to Walworth Road where he was soon shopping for shoes and clothes.

'Just got paid, sir?' a shop assistant asked. 'Can't be a better day to treat yourself.'

Tee laughed as he handed over some money. The assistant thought he was laughing at his silly joke, but Tee was in fact laughing because he saw the name on the pay packet.

That night when Tee got home to sister Pearl's, Girlie was in bed and glad to see him. Tee had a bath and then climbed in with Girlie, and they loved the dark hours away until they fell into a deep sleep.

From then on, Tee devoted himself to creeping. Sometimes he found he had taken cheque-books and cheque cards on his rounds, and he sold these for a bit of money to the kiters who knew how to use them. It was a girl named Melissa who showed him there was more to be made from these finds than he had realised.

Melissa had heard Tee had cheque-books and cards for sale.

'I need a cheque-book and card fast to do some work,' she told him. 'Things are awful at home and I left my son to come and search for one.'

Now it just happened that Tee could help. They were standing on the Front Line, outside a cab shop. Tee asked her to come inside and when they were safely behind the doors, he took a Midland cheque-book and card out of his pocket.

'Is this what you need?' he asked.

'Yeah, man,' she answered, her face lighting up like a Christmas tree. 'Let me see.' She muttered that the card needed cleaning. 'Come on, we'll go to my place,' she said.

They made their way to a big house on Clapham Common North Side, and went up to Melissa's one-bedroom flat on the top floor. Melissa told the baby-sitter, who was looking after her son, to hold tight for a bit longer if she wanted to get a treat.

Melissa and Tee went into the bathroom to clean the card. She had a tin of brake fluid and some nail-polish remover and she mixed the two together and placed the card, bearing the signature of the real owner, into the liquid. She left it to soak while they shared a joint Tee had rolled, and when they had finished it they looked into the saucer. The mixture had completely lifted the signature from the card. Melissa wasted no time in replacing it with one in her own handwriting and within an hour they were shopping in Croydon. With the newly signed card, she could draw fifty

137

pounds a cheque from each bank and she did just that. Tee bought a suit, a pair of shoes and an overcoat, and Melissa got herself and her son the food and clothes they needed. They had spent almost £200 between them. On the way home they stopped at an off-licence and used the money that was left to buy drink, some of which Melissa could sell later.

By the time they returned to the flat in Clapham, Tee had learned a useful lesson. If Melissa could do cheque-book fraud, then so could he. Within days, he was pulling in more money than ever.

That summer Girlie told Tee she was going to have his baby. He was happier than he had ever been. They had put their names on the list for council flats and it seemed that for the first time since he was a small boy he would have a proper family and a home of his own. But it also meant Tee would need money for prams, cots, the lot. At the same time, he wanted to get himself a car. Not just any car but one like all the big men on the Front Line drove – something flashy, fast, smooth. So he kept on getting money any way he could, committing more and more and more crimes.

Sometimes he tried dealing in weed on the Front Line, by buying a ten-pound bag, dividing it into three and selling each one on for ten pounds. But this was slow going, and Tee was soon looking for quicker ways of getting some of the drug money.

One day while he was hanging about on the Front Line, he heard a man asking where he could get ten ounces of black hash. He was a likely-looking victim, and Tee went straight over and said he could get it. The man looked at him suspiciously, so Tee went around the street borrowing as much money as he could from all his friends and then stood ostentatiously counting all his money, showing the punter he was serious. Eventually, the punter came over. The trap was now set.

A price of £90 an ounce was agreed, plus an extra £100 that Tee insisted was for his commission – he thought this was a nice touch, as he meant to keep the whole lot. The punter handed over £1,000 and Tee put it in his pocket and walked nonchalantly around the corner. Once out of sight he made a hasty exit, leaving the punter with nothing. It was as simple as that. Later on that evening Tee paid back the friends he had borrowed from, with a little extra, got some weed for himself and then went home. Girlie was in, relaxing, and Roland was there too. 'I wrote a new song,' he said. 'Want to hear it?'

'Sing it, mek me hear no,' Tee replied.

When Roland sang his song, Tee said he thought it was great, and that night everyone was happy. It seemed the future could only bring more of the same.

Another time, Tee played a similar trick, only this time he pretended to be the punter. Carrying a loaded sports bag, he went into a pub well known for drug deals and asked where he could buy ten kilos of Jamaican Sensimilia weed. At first no one took the bait, but then a shifty-looking man came up to Tee while he was having a slash. He checked that there was no one else in the toilets before he said, 'Me can sell you some weed, but it's not Sess.'

'No me no want no African weed,' said Tee, playing hard to get. 'Me want Sess.'

'Me can take you and show you it still?'

'Me not sure,' Tee said apparently reluctant, as he sussed him out. The man was clearly desperate to do a deal, and he wouldn't be any trouble to rip off.

'Yeah, man, it no far get a cab.'

Tee allowed himself to be persuaded. He found a cab

and they drove back to the man's house, where he asked the driver to wait. The man produced the weed and Tee looked it over and put it in his bag. Then he simply pushed open the front door, walked out into the street, climbed into the cab and drove off. It was as easy as taking candy from kids.

That night when he got home, loaded with money from selling on the weed, Girlie was as sweet as ever. Her belly was enormous by now. 'We got a letter from the council,' she said. 'All we have to do is collect the key and rent book for our new flat.'

First thing the next morning they fetched the key and went to look at the flat, which was in the Surrey Docks. This area was frequented by the National Front, but Tee wasn't worried – all he was interested in was looking after his woman and child. And it was a nice flat, with two bedrooms. They were both looking forward to moving in, but they decided they should wait until the baby was born, as Kellett Road was so near the hospital. Girlie and Tee spent the whole of that night and the next day together.

Tee had been making serious money over the last few months, what with his drug-dealing and all his other crimes, and even after giving Girlie money for baby things and furniture, he found he still had enough to fulfil one of his greatest dreams – buying a car with enough style to fit his image.

Luckily enough, just a couple of days earlier he had heard about a Jensen Interceptor for sale. He wasted no time in phoning the owner, who invited him to come and view the car. It was a beautiful beige vehicle, and when Tee opened the door and sat on the soft white leather seats and smelt the sweet smell it gave off, he knew this was *the* car. Then he looked up and opened the sun roof. It worked perfectly. The owner showed

Tee the lever near the accelerator pedal which you pulled to open the boot, and the catch that released the bonnet.

Tee got out and looked over the engine. It was clean and new. Then he got back in and turned the key, and it started up crisply on the first attempt. The engine roared when he pressed the accelerator pedal and made the car sound like a real road-hog.

'Want to take it for a spin?' asked the man.

'Yeah!' said Tee. There was nothing he wanted more.

The owner got in and Tee drove the car away from the kerb. It was fast! But it wasn't until Tee was on a long road and the owner said, 'Kick the pedal down,' that he saw how the car shot off like a bullet.

'Wow!' he said.

'Exactly, son. Drive this car carefully, the kick down is fast.'

Tee could not hide the fact that he had already fallen in love with the car and the owner could see it clearly.

When they returned to the house, Tee paid over all the rest of his cash and drove the Jensen away with a smile on his face. When he got to the Front Line, everyone stopped to admire it as he went by. Tee just sat back, at ease, loving the feel and the sound of the classic car. He didn't have a driving licence or any insurance, but that didn't matter. Now he was really going places.

He couldn't wait to get home to show Girlie, and when he did she was thrilled with the car too. They drove all over Brixton, and finally dropped off some furniture Girlie had bought at their new flat.

Autumn turned to winter. It was very cold and the snow started falling around the middle of December. The baby was due any day and Girlie's belly was so big they wondered if she was expecting twins, but

Christmas Day came and went, and she was still carrying. Tee spent every moment, day and night, with her, loving her and reassuring her that everything would be all right, while outside the snow covered South London like a thick carpet.

But one night there was a big dance down at Waterloo town hall. Everyone was set on being there, including Roland, and though Tee didn't feel like leaving Girlie, she insisted that he go out. Roland and Tee climbed into the Jensen and drove off into the night. It was about one in the morning when they got to the hall. The doormen were old friends, and let them in for free. Inside, a sound system was full on and the dance was swinging. There were blacks, whites, Rasta men, Indians, and all sorts there, all jumping and skanking, drinking and smoking. The smell of weed filled the air. At the end of the smaller hall was the bar where all the big and respected bad men stood with their women, drinking champagne, smoking big joints and snorting coke – men like the great Boy Blue, who was wearing a blue suit with a heavy gold chain around his neck that ended in a wicked-looking large gold scorpion. Boy Blue's chin rested on his hand and Tee could see all the gold and diamonds on his fingers, one of which permanently pointed straight out. A thin, long scar ran down one side of his face. Beside him was his girl, Jan, a red-skinned half-caste queen, draped in gold and dressed in rude-girl clothes. She made every male in that dancehall jealous, posing, laughing and fussing over her man.

Tee looked on. He had his Jensen, but he knew he still wasn't a touch on Boy Blue. He moved on to another section of the dance where he saw all the Rebels with their queens and princesses. Girlie was now on Tee's mind again, and he walked over to Roland who was smoking a big spliff.

'Wha you ah seh, Pupatee?' Roland asked.

'You ready, star,' Tee replied. 'Ca wha Girlie could ah be giving birth by now.'

'Ah true rude bwoy, come we steps no?'

'Ah no lie,' he said.

'All right, people, different style, different fashion,' were the last words they heard from the DJ on the sound system on their way out. They jumped in the Jensen and as they pulled up at Kellett Road, Tee saw the lights were off in Girlie's room. He felt relieved because she must be asleep, but he had hardly got through the front door when Pearl told him that Girlie's water had burst and Selena had gone with her in an ambulance to King's College Hospital.

In no time at all Tee had followed her, and was with Girlie while she gave birth. It wasn't an easy job but he did what he could to help, talking and encouraging, and eventually she delivered a beautiful baby. 'It's a little girl,' the midwife called. Girlie held her daughter to her chest and smiled up at him.

It was December 1977 and London was white with snow, and icy cold. Tee visited Girlie and the baby daily until they were given permission to leave the hospital, and when that day came he picked them up and drove them back to Kellett Road, where Tee's family all joined in a small celebration. The baby was named Paulette, and everyone loved her straight away. Tee and Girlie also had to take Paulette round to see Girlie's parents, but Tee didn't look forward to this, much as he had been longing to show his daughters to his own family. Mr and Mrs Fryer did not like Tee, and had not approved of Girlie taking up with him; they had particularly not approved of her getting

143

pregnant by him. Mr Fryer, Girlie's stepfather, had even tried to persuade her to have an abortion. (Both Mr and Mrs Fryer were white, for Girlie's real father, who was black, had run out on the family when she was quite young.) But now that they actually saw the baby, they could not hold back their delight. They cradled Paulette in their arms and cooed over her, and Girlie felt happy to have made peace with them again.

When everyone had been shown the baby, Tee drove Girlie and Paulette to the new flat in Surrey Docks. He had moved all their gear in while Girlie was still in hospital, so they were able to stay there that night, the first in their new home.

This was it at last. Tee had a family of his own, and now he had to listen to Girlie's pleas for him to lead a responsible life and find a job. So he put his Jensen away in a garage and bought himself an old mashed-up Cortina – an honest car for an honest man – and started asking around about work. It wasn't easy, for Tee did not have much to offer, and after a few days he felt very discouraged and almost gave up and got the Jensen back out. But then he met two old friends, Lloydy and Jimmy, who were brothers. They were working together on a building site in the City of London. Their boss had mentioned that he was looking for labourers so they suggested Tee go along and have an interview. He had learned a bit about bricklaying in borstal, which might help. To his delight, the interview went well and he was offered the job, starting the following week.

Tee turned up on time on the Monday morning. It was a big building site, with several blocks of flats being erected over a large area, and the labourers were divided into teams. Tee was assigned to a black foreman called Alford, and Lloydy and Jimmy were on

144

the same team. Alford turned out to be a good boss, quick with a smile and never demanding more than a man could give. Tee's first task was to clean up the mess left by the bricklayers, carpenters, plasterers and other skilled workers in one of the flats which was nearly finished so that the electricians could come in and wire up.

'Huh,' he thought to himself, 'bad bwoy Tee become a rubbisher sweeper!' But then he remembered his loving Girlie and his beautiful daughter Paulette, and got on with the job. He worked his way through the flat, putting his back into it, so that when he got to the final room he was knackered and filthy and drenched with sweat. But when Alford came to inspect, he saw Tee had done a good job. 'Blood claat, Tee, you do dem good, man!' he said, and Tee felt as proud as he had ever done pulling off a good touch in a shop or on the earth.

The work continued through the morning, and when they finally had a rest, Tee decided he needed a joint to relax him. Alford was making himself a roll-up, so Tee borrowed a Rizla and started putting weed and hash in to make a cocktail.

'What you have deh, ganja?' Alford asked. He came over and looked for himself. 'Blood claat, ah good weed you have man, you ah sell any?'

'How much you want?' Tee asked reluctantly.

'Me will take ah twenty pound draw off you till then?'

Tee stopped to consider this, but Alford went on at him. 'Come on, Tee man. Oh God, man, and de weed look so good!'

Tee took out a bookie paper which he used to store small amounts of weed, and gave it to Alford without a word.

The next day when Tee turned up for work, his job

was to bring plasterboards down from one lot of flats to another.

'Plasterboard,' he said, glumly, knowing how heavy they were.

'Ah easy job, man,' Alford assured him. 'You just put dem pon de dumper truck, and tie dem down and take you time, drive dem over.'

'Oh dat sound better.'

'When you reach over de new flats some other men will be there to take dem off and take dem in de flat, ah easy work, man.'

So Tee spent that day carrying down the plasterboards and driving the dumper truck, and at the end of the day, he cleaned himself up and went home to Girlie and Paulette in their little flat in Surrey Docks.

On other days, Tee worked with the floor-layer, filling up the wheelbarrow with mixed concrete and taking it to him, or he carried the hod for the brickies, or did other labouring jobs. He was grateful for his size and strength.

Since Alford had bought the weed from him, other workers started asking for some, and these sales supplemented Tee's wages, which came to about £120 a week.

But it was not an easy life. Tee missed his old freedoms, and Girlie did, too. She was a poor cook and a worse housekeeper, and as the dust built up, the flat grew dirtier and dirtier. Girlie felt trapped and lonely. If this was life with a kid, she said, she certainly wasn't going to have any more, and she put herself on the pill. She was very excited about these pills, as if they were something addictive. She also grew very skinny, but still maintained her beauty.

By now, work was getting the better of Tee, too. Sometimes his old friends would drive by in their smart cars and call up to him, asking what he was doing. 'De great Tee ah work like a slave,' they would say. 'Stop dat, man, and come and do some big robberies with we. You can't make no money ah work fe white man, star. Ah foolishness dat, Tee, God know.'

Tee tried not to listen, and told them that he was finished with jail. Then some would say, 'Ah true,' but others would reply, 'Go weh! Ah soft you ah get, soft, man.' Tee began to spend more of his wages on doing up his Jensen, which he kept getting out from the garage, or some other little luxury to make him feel better; this didn't please Girlie, who was stuck in the flat with Paulette and had no money to buy things for herself.

At least Mr and Mrs Fryer came to the rescue, at the weekends. They would look after Paulette while Tee and Girlie climbed into the Jensen and drove down Streatham Hill. Girlie could still drink like a fish and when she was ready to enjoy herself Tee desired her more than ever.

But during the week, things went from bad to worse. Sometimes Tee noticed that Girlie's life was a bit of an ordeal, washing and cooking and cleaning and looking after the baby, but he couldn't see what he could do about it, and anyway, he thought, Girlie must have realised what she was getting herself into when she got pregnant. Then one day, Tee was almost killed on the building site when a girder fell and landed only a foot away from him. He went home in a state of shock, thinking about life and death, and found the flat in a state of chaos. It was filthy, there was no food in the fridge, and Paulette was crying, with a dirty nappy on and no one to look after her. After a frantic search Tee eventually found Girlie in the next-door flat, drinking tea and laughing happily with a neighbour.

147

That evening, Tee and Girlie had a big argument, and the next day, he gave up his job, took out his Jensen Interceptor, and drove down to the Front Line.

He was back into a life of crime, robbing, conning, making money however he could, and now that he had cash to spend again, Tee's eyes began to wander. One night at a party he met a young woman called Lorna whom he had known from years before, and he ended up staying over at her flat.

Girlie was furious when he went back to her the next morning, but after screaming at him for a bit she burst into tears. She already felt he had let her down by giving up his job. Tee assured her that his heart belonged to her – and he really did love Girlie – but the truth was that he was always looking for some new excitement.

Girlie and Tee still spent the occasional good weekend together, but in general things were going from bad to worse. Arguments grew into fights, and to his shame she sometimes got the worst of these. Neither of them was even twenty years old; they had taken on family life without realising what they were getting into, and both of them were fed up with it. But when Girlie talked about separating, Tee's heart would melt and he would hold her and kiss her and love her up, telling her not to be silly, and they would be loving again until Tee stayed out another few nights, or Girlie abandoned Paulette, and then the fighting would start up again.

Tee tried not to see too much of Lorna, because of Girlie, but he couldn't help himself. Lorna loved to go out clubbing and she had as much energy in bed as on the dance floor. Although she lived with her mum, he had a green light to stay there whenever he wanted, and he was happy to get no sleep if it was Lorna, rather than Paulette, keeping him awake. And if that wasn't enough, he also began to see another girl from the old times, a dark beauty named Princess. Tee now had three women and a Jensen Interceptor to support, and he needed money, lots of it.

One day he snatched a bag which by good fortune turned out to have £1,500 in it, but when he was running away a couple of idiots who knew him shouted out his name. That evening, some police officers stopped Tee and said his name had been mentioned in connection with the snatching. He was put on an ID parade, but fortunately he had changed clothes and was not picked out.

When he got back on to the streets, he was in a seriously bad mood. He walked around telling people in Brixton that they could call him anything they liked, but he was not going to have his name shouted out in the streets. That night, still feeling angry and fed up, he ran into some of the lads he had been with when he was arrested on the tube before being sent to Aylesbury. They were draped in gold jewellery and flashing their wealth. He reminded them that he had gone down for thefts they had all committed, and that he hadn't grassed them up; not only had they repaid him by never coming to visit him in prison, they hadn't even sent a fiver into his private spends account. 'Now me ah see you all in ah pure big gold,' he said. While he spoke, his fury and sense of injustice rose until he could contain himself no more, and he pulled out his knife and relieved them of all their rings, diamonds, rope chains and everything else. They didn't even try to resist him. 'And you all better tink yourself lucky me no plunge up couple ah you,' he said. The only one he didn't rob was B, who had been sent to borstal.

For all his problems supporting the women he already had, it wasn't long before Tee had got himself involved with Karen, a blue-eyed blonde whom he met at a club. Now he had Girlie and Paulette, Lorna, Princess and Karen, and he couldn't let go of any of them, he liked them all too much. Although he felt that his life was spinning out of control, going from one woman to the next, if he saw another dazzler in the street, he couldn't help going after this new one as well.

Princess was now his favourite. She would tell him about her wealthy mother who lived abroad. She planned to go and live with her. 'When dat day deh come,' Tee would tell her, 'me ah go miss you.' But Lorna and he were also getting closer, and Lorna was now starting to talk about having children. 'Let's have five and they'll grow up to be singer superstars like the Jacksons,' she would say. If he ran into her while he was out with one of his other women, she would wave at him across the crowd and shout, 'Oh, yeah, Tee.' Then she would cross the street and put her lips to his ear and whisper, 'Are you taking me home tonight darling?', the hot breath from her wet lips caressing his ear. It was impossible not to turn round and say, 'Why of course, honey.'

When he went back to see Girlie, she would say, 'Hiya stranger,' and try to look happy. Paulette was now getting bigger and stronger, but Girlie was very unhappy. She would break down and cry. 'What's wrong?' he would ask. 'Nothing,' she would reply. He would hold her and kiss her and tell her not to worry. He would take her for a drive and a smoke and slowly she would come round, but never for very long.

That year, things were hotting up in Brixton. One of the toughest young firms on the street was run by

Dennis and Dirty, with their girls, Evonne and toothless Dorothy. At that time there were also a couple of policemen, Wickens and Chapman, whose aim it was to make life difficult for the neighbourhood criminals. One night they made the mistake of messing with Dennis and Dirty and their firm, and ended up in hospital. Of course the policemen knew who had assaulted them, and so the members of the firm were all on the run. But that was nothing new in Brixton.

That year, too, Tee's old friend Barry Black, who was doing eight years for a string of robberies on milkmen, died in prison, and it was rumoured the screws had killed him.

Tee was now committing crimes at will. If he saw someone wearing something he liked, he would simply say, 'Ho, your chops is nice, mek me try dat on, no.' Then he would add, 'Mek ah hold ah couple days' wear of dis, no,' and whether they said yes or no made no difference. If they said no, he would reply, 'You too mean, man.' If they said nothing, he would say, 'Nice one, man,' and walk away. With this little trick, he soon ended up looking like a walking jewellery shop, and Girlie and his other women were covered in gold too.

Tee had now been out of prison for two years, the longest period of freedom since he was first sent away at the age of thirteen. He believed he was invincible. He was never going back to jail. But at the end of 1978, he was arrested for pickpocketing and though he was let off with a big fine, it shook him up. He felt pickpocketing had too many risks without enough gains. He had to do something a bit smarter.

It was at this time he met up again with Blakie and Roderick, two of his old friends from the Brixton Rebels. They were robbers but not very successful, and they were looking for a third to join their crew – someone big and strong and fearless, someone, in fact, like Tee. Early one morning, Blakie and Roderick called around at Tee's in a stolen Ford Capri, and suggested he go along with them on a day's crime spree. Tee was ready for something like this, and agreed immediately. He climbed into the car. Blakie asked what he had with him, and Tee pulled out a flick-knife. Roderick in turn showed his cutlass, while Blakie pulled out a big long .45 handgun.

They drove off and headed for Croydon, where Roderick and Tee ended up walking armed into a jewellery shop on the high street. Roderick had the .45 and he waved it in the air and shouted at the jeweller and his assistant, 'Don't blood claat move or try a ting or you both dead fast. Where is all the money, get it fast or you'll both pick one each out of this gun in your fucking face!'

Tee had pulled out his knife, which was long enough to run a man clean through. The jeweller opened a drawer and, leaning over, Tee saw that inside were stacks of notes. He pulled a bag from his pocket and reached over and began stuffing all the money inside it. He grabbed a case, which contained gold. At the same time, Roderick was wasting no time filling another bag with gold and jewels from the displays. It was only a matter of seconds before Roderick ordered the two men into the back of the shop and he and Tee ran out, jumped into the waiting car, and were gone.

When they divided up the money, it came to five grand between the three of them, not to mention the gold they had taken. Tee felt delighted. This was much better than working on the building site for £120 a week. He and Roderick and Blakie agreed to work together from then on.

There was no need to do anything for a while, with all the money they had made, but eventually that was used up and it was time to head out again. This time, Blakie was ill, so Roderick brought along another man, Johnny White, to be the driver. That day was more sobering for Tee. Nothing seemed to go right. They first tried a supermarket in Wimbledon, wandering around looking for an opportunity. But they couldn't see one, so they left. As they walked back down the street towards their Ford, a police car pulled up. Someone in the supermarket must have called the cops, because the two policemen questioned them about what they had been doing in there. Fortunately, they didn't bother to search them, as Roderick had the .45 down his back, Tee had his knife, and in the car, Johnny had a .38 handgun. When the police let them go, the three of them went back to the car and they drove out of Wimbledon and went home penniless, but at least without a court hearing ahead of them.

The pattern was now set, and whenever they ran short of money Blakie and Roderick and Tee would meet up and try some form of robbery or other. Sometimes it was shops, other times it was stealing from drug dealers – this could be more dangerous physically, but at least it didn't usually have the risk of a jail sentence at the end. If they heard of someone holding a big enough quantity of coke or heroin or weed or hash they would make arrangements to meet and view the goods, and then simply pull out their weapons and walk away with the drugs.

It was a hit-and-miss profession. On one occasion, they heard about a dealer in Tottenham selling coke. They called up and arranged to buy three kilos. When they got to the meeting place, they tested the coke and found it to be good stuff. They produced an attaché case and lifted up the lid, showing the piles of notes. In fact the piles were blank paper, and only the top notes were real money, but this view was enough to make the dealer and his friends salivate, and they went out and returned with the three kilos. Blakie picked up the coke and put it down his trousers, Roderick pulled out the .45 and ordered the dealers into another room, and they walked out as calm as anything, to celebrate their great success – only to discover that the men they had robbed had been planning to rob them, and had cut the coke so it was more like one kilo than three. Nevertheless, this was still a lot of coke, and the three robbers divided it up and set about selling their shares.

One night, around this time, Tee ended up at a party with Natty D, Dirty H, Pete and a few other friends. They decided to step outside to get some fresh air when an older man pushed Pete as he came past, saying, 'Bwoy, move outa de way.'

Pete exchanged a few words with the man who was soon threatening him. Tee joined in, saying, 'Yeah, Pete, take him outside, let we gang him and bust up him, claat.' The man started on him and asked if he wanted war.

'Of course,' said Tee. 'What you think we going to do?'

They walked outside, the man breathing down Tee's neck. Tee suddenly started to throw lefts and rights to his chin. The man wasn't even throwing punches, just trying to keep on his feet. The fight carried on down the pavement until they came to a jeweller's shop. In the heat of the action, Tee gave the man a flying jump kick and he shot back against the window of the jeweller's, shattering it. Tee picked him out of the glass and gave him some more kicks and head-butts and rights and lefts until he was out cold. Then Tee noticed another man reaching in to the shop to grab some of the gold, so he ran over and lifted him up by his shirt collar with both arms and told him to beat it, these were his takings. Then he let him go and started filling his pockets. By this stage, all his friends had gathered round and were looking at him with their mouths open. 'Nobody don't want no gold?' he asked. Then hell broke loose as everybody grabbed what they could.

The next day the whole of Brixton was talking about the previous night's events. 'Did you see the way Tee drape up that man who tried to steal the gold?' someone said. 'Yeah, drape up! That's what they should call Tee, Drape Up.' He took the name as a compliment and even made it part of his practice to lift up, or drape up, people when he robbed them.

In the summer of 1979, his girlfriend Karen told him she was pregnant. 'Don't leave me,' she said when she told him. 'I didn't mean to get pregnant. Can't you just punch me in the belly to make me lose it?'

Tee took her in his arms and said, 'Hey babe, I'm happy you're having a baby and I'm not going to leave you. We're both going to love the little child when you give birth.'

She smiled with happiness and held him close and they ended up making love all that night.

Girlie must have known about his other women, for apart from being away all the time he would sometimes call out other names in his sleep. But though Girlie quizzed him about this, she never really pushed him. And by now he had added another girl to his list, a plump Indian named Iley. He couldn't stop. He was women crazy. Every time he managed to get away from one woman he would jump in his car and drive to another. He was driving fast, but heading nowhere good.

7

Return to Jamaica

In the midst of all this, as Christmas drew near again, Tee received news that his brother Gamper, who was living in America with his wife, had been killed in a road accident. Tee had not seen Gamper for many years, but the news hit him badly, and he kept thinking back to how Gamper and his friends had saved him when he was drowning in that river years before.

The first thing that came into his mind was getting to Jamaica, where Gamper's funeral was going to be held. But he was broke. He was still hanging out with Blakie and Roderick, and they were still working armed robberies, but they were not having much luck and their last job had only netted them a couple of hundred pounds. But when Tee told his partners about his predicament they were very sympathetic, and they stole a Ford Escort as a getaway car and drove all round London, looking for an easy touch. As they drove, Tee grew sadder and more worried that he wouldn't be able to be beside Gamper as he left the world of light and disappeared into the world of darkness.

Eventually, they left London, looking for some

small-town target, and by the time they drove into the centre of a town it was already getting late. Tee was praying that they would get a touch here. 'Mek me skout out one ah dem shops fore we call it ah day?' Roderick suggested and they all agreed. They decided on a likely-looking gift shop.

They parked the stolen Ford a couple of blocks away, and Tee was the first out of the car, the first to the top of the road, and the first to enter the store. He walked around the shop but secretly looked through a half-open door into a back room where he saw a man sorting through piles of money on a table in front of him. It was the Christmas takings! Tee's eyes almost popped out of his head. He pushed open the door and walked into the room. The man looked up, and his mouth fell open in shock and horror as he saw Tee's big knife.

Tee walked forward. He pulled out a big white carrier bag from his pocket and began to stuff the money inside. The man stood up and opened his mouth as if to make a protest, but Tee gave him a shove and he fell to the floor like a sack of potatoes. But instead of lying there as Tee had expected, the man scrambled to his feet and ran past him out of the door as if he was turbo charged. Tee barely noticed, he was so excited by all the money. He stuffed the rest of it in the bag, except for two piles of twenty-pound notes, which he hid in his underpants on account of his particular needs and the fact that Blakie and Roderick were still nowhere to be seen. But when he turned to leave, he was confronted by the man who had run away returning with a couple of assistants.

Fortunately, behind them, he also saw Blakie and Roderick. 'Money to rass claat!' Tee shouted and Blakie and Roderick drew their big knives as he ran towards them. The men who were following him saw this and

157

screeched to a halt. They charged in the other direction, knocking goods off the shelves and making a terrible noise. The robbers walked out of the store as cool as they could and then turned the corner and sprinted up the block to where their car was parked. Roderick was the fastest runner, and by the time Blakie and Tee got there the car was already started and the doors open. They dived in and Roderick skidded off and out of there as fast as he could. A few miles away they came to a train station, and they abandoned the car and walked calmly in and bought their tickets and took the train back to London. When they were safely home, they counted the money and found they had £1,800 each.

They were all pleased with the haul, but Roderick was so delighted he couldn't stop laughing and throwing his money in the air.

'I'll slip away,' Tee said. 'I've got things to do.'

'Yeah, nice man, later Drape Up,' Roderick replied.

Later, when he added in what he had stuffed down his underpants, Tee discovered he had a total of three grand. He stashed most of the money and took a few hundred pounds and sorted Girlie out. Then he drove to see Karen and sorted her out. By the end of the evening, he must have sorted everyone out even if only with a drink or food or some cigarettes, and he ended up that night at a club where he got stoned and nicely drunk.

The next day he went and booked himself on the first flight he could, which was five days away, two days after Christmas, hoping he would make it back to Jamaica not too long after Gamper, who was being flown there in a casket.

He went out and bought presents for the family he had not seen for so many years, including a beautiful dress for Mama which would make her look like a queen. When the day came, he took a cab out to the airport. It was a long flight and on the way the plane stopped in Bermuda, from where Tee sent postcards to Girlie and Karen and other people in England. Then they took off on the last leg of the journey and before long, as Tee was anticipating the great welcome he would get, the plane began to descend over Jamaica, towards Norman Manley airport. Below them, the sun was sparkling on the sea. When the doors opened and he stepped outside, the warm sticky air hit him like the breath of a giant.

Tee collected his luggage and walked through the doors to be greeted by his sister Jeanie and her husband Joseph. After they had laughed awkwardly and then hugged each other, he looked around at all the other people being reunited. Up above them was a balcony, and standing there, watching everyone like hawks, was a group of men who looked just like the bad bwoys he hung around with in Brixton.

When Jeanie saw what he was looking at she cried, 'Lord God, Joseph, no bad bwoy so-and-so and him tiefing friends dem dat? Jesus Christ, hurry up and tek we way from here, you hear, for me no able fe dem try robbed and kill us ya!'

'Just relax and cool man, ah me name ranking! No, bwoy, can't test dis,' said Joseph. He was a tall, slim, dark-skinned man with more brains than strength.

It was about forty-five minutes' drive to Chapelton, the small town where Joseph and Jeanie lived with their baby daughter Sakasher. On the way they passed through Spanish Town, where they told him Carl was now living. Tee couldn't wait to see his brother again. As they drove on, Tee noticed the lush greens of the countryside around him, and how brightly coloured

159

people's clothes were. Joseph waved at passers-by who smiled and saluted back. It all seemed so small. The bright sun made Tee squint and his shirt was sticking to his back, but he breathed the air in deeply through the open window. Jamaica was his old home, and yet he couldn't help feeling like a tourist.

When they arrived, Tee stretched himself out on the veranda.

'Pupatee?' Jeanie called to him.

'Yes, sister.'

'Wha you want fe eat?'

'Anyting, man, me just no eat pork.'

'Joseph, go kill two chicken fe me no do, darling.'

'Ah no nutting dat man, it dun already,' he said as he left to carry out the request.

Tee lifted up the baby and looked at her. She was about the same age as his daughter Paulette.

'Tomorrow Joseph will take you over to see Mama and Pops,' Jeanie said. 'Come on, I'll show you your room.'

When they came back down, he tried to give Jeanie some money, but she refused. She was the youngest of all his sisters and without doubt the most beautiful. She was also very educated, as she was a school teacher.

'You want some orange?' Joseph asked him when he came back with the chicken.

'Yeah, man.'

They walked outside and there were three orange trees hung with big fat fruit. He reached up and picked one, and when he ate some it was sweet and fresh. He took another one and he kept picking and peeling and eating orange after orange.

'How long you in Jamaica for?' Joseph asked.

'Six weeks,' he said. Then he asked, 'When ah Gamper's funeral?'

160

'Your sister no tell you? You miss de funeral.'

'No?'

'Yeah, man, dem buried him couple days ago. It was a big funeral, everybody was there man.'

Tee was shocked and sad that he had missed the funeral. He had come all this way specially to see his brother buried, and suddenly he realised how long it had been since they had last seen each other. But at least he was in Jamaica and he could put some flowers on his grave and have a talk to him, whatever good it would do.

When they got back into the house there was a strong smell of curried chicken and Tee's mouth was watering.

'Pupatee, you want rice or bread with de chicken?'

'Me no mind you know, sister,' he replied.

While he was waiting for dinner, Joseph took him into the front room and opened the bar, where there were bottles of red and white rum, brandy, wine, stout, Heineken and soft drinks. Tee tried some white rum first, which set his throat and belly aflame and his head spinning. By the time dinner was ready he was almost drunk and twice as hungry. His sister placed in front of him a large bowl of chicken and gravy, and another bowl of rice, and another with calaloo. To drink, there was a large glass jug filled with iced grapefruit punch. Joseph turned on the radio and Tee ate listening to classical reggae and the Jamaican news station, as content as he could be. He was home.

The following morning, Joseph and he set off to visit Tee's parents. It was a hard drive, followed by a long walk from the end of the road. They crossed rivers and climbed hills, and finally came to familiar landmarks. Here was the river where Gamper had rescued Tee. It still looked dangerous, but Tee was a good swimmer now and he looked forward to taking a plunge.

'By the way, Pupatee, you smoke ganja?' Joseph said.

'Yeah, man,' Tee replied. 'I'm dying for a spliff.'

'You should of tell me cause we did past de place where dem sell it. Anyway, me have couple ah fifty-cent sticks,' he said, handing Tee one.

They climbed a little hill and there below them was the house Tee had grown up in. He was filled with excitement. His mother was standing on the veranda, looking up at them. He rushed down to the house and took her in his arms and kissed her and hugged her. 'Let me see you face,' she said, but he just kept holding her in his arms. When finally he stepped back to take a look at her, she was smaller than he remembered: slim and strong and dark. He tried to look his best for her, putting on the most angelic smile he could, for she was a God-fearing woman.

'So you come to see Mama, Pupatee,' she said. 'You brother Gamper dead. You know dem bury him couple days ago, see him grave deh in de back.' She pointed and he saw a neat grave.

'Where is Pops and everyone else, Mama?' Tee asked.

'You father gone down ah British market. From you left when you was a little boy till now him no miss a Saturday when him no go British market. You will see him later. You brother Carl work ah Spanish town driving taxi car. You sister Ivy big son Ervin turn bad man and live down ah British side. Ah just me and you father plus you brother dead and left pickneys live here now son.' She turned and shouted, 'Hedward, Barry. Come meet you uncle.'

'Yes, Granny,' small voices responded, and two boys ran out of the sugar-cane field, eating cane.

'Howdy, Uncle Pupatee,' they said, and Tee saw that they looked just like Gamper.

162

Joseph said he had to go and conduct some business and Mama told Edward and Barry to collect firewood, leaving her and Tee to talk. He told her how everyone was in England, and then gave her £200. He said he was going to give the same to Pops.

'You better just give him £100,' she said. 'You know how him drink de white rum and go on bad when him ready.'

Tee looked at her in surprise, but she shook her head. 'Him still de same, him no change. We even have to sleep in different room and bed, because him too rude!'

Tee gave her the dress he had bought for her. It was a bit big but she was thrilled and held it up to her asking how she looked. Then she burst into tears, and said how happy she was to see her wash-belly son now he was grown. He wondered how much she knew about his activities in Brixton, but she didn't ask.

Eventually Mama set about making dinner for them all: saltfish and ackee, yams, green bananas, sweet potatoes, dumplings and coco. The food of his childhood.

When it grew dark, Tee began to get impatient to see his father. Suddenly he saw the outline of a figure on a horse on top of the hill and he walked up to meet him. Pops looked down at Tee, screwing his eyes up in the darkness.

'Wha happen, Pops?' said Tee.

The old man looked at him good. 'Ah Pupatee?'

'Yeah man, ah Pupatee.'

'Den how you look like Carl so?'

Pops got off his horse and they shook hands and walked together down to the house. Tee could see that his father had shrunk. He was half the size he had been, the muscles thinned out.

'Papa, you see our son come look fe we?' Mama said.

163

'So me ah see, Ma.'

'You want some food?'

'Yes, tanks.'

When he was finished eating, Pops had a bit of food left on his plate. 'Hedward and Barry!' he called. 'You can have dis if you want.' The two boys smiled and took the food aside and began eating. Tee gave Pops £150, which he took and thanked him for. It was late now and very dark, as it had been when Tee was young. There was still no electricity in this part of Jamaica. Pops and he washed their feet and said good-night.

In the morning, the cock-a-doodle-doo of the rooster woke Tee and for a moment he thought he was a boy again, waking in the only house he knew. Mama was soon up and in the kitchen, and Pops followed shortly afterwards. When the two boys appeared, rubbing the sleep from their eyes, Tee smiled as he remembered back to when Carl and he had been just like them. It was good to be home again.

Tee walked around the house. Mama was boiling coffee and frying dumplings and eggs and plantain. Then he strode outside. Edward and Barry were chopping wood, and down below the large cherry tree, Pops was milking a cow. Tee went down and helped him until they had a whole bucket to take back up to the kitchen. 'It good to see you again, man,' Pops said. 'Specially with you brother Gamper who just get buried.' Tee couldn't find the words to show his sorrow so he just nodded.

Eventually he said, 'What we doing today?'

'Me going to pad up two donkeys and two mules and go cut some grass down where you grandfather did buried and put the grass away. When me come back and feed de milking cows little every night. Me can't cut de grass every day in me old age, me son.'

164

'No worry yourself, man. Me ah look forward fe do de most work today, Pops.'

After breakfast, Pops and Tee walked with the donkeys and mules about three miles down to a hill with tall grass. Tee took two of the animals and climbed up the hill to where the grass was out in the open with the blazing sun right on it. He cut the grass quickly and tied it into large bundles and was soon leading the animals back down to where his father was working. He had cut plenty of grass, so Tee bundled that up too, and they cut and bundled together for many hours. When they were finished, Tee took out his cigarette. His father asked for one.

'Me never know you smoke, Pops?'

'Yeah, man, me smoke, man.'

On the way back they saw some boys fishing on the river bank.

'Catch any fish?' his father called to them. The boys smiled and bent down and lifted from the water two long sticks which had plenty of fish on them. Tee remembered how much Mama and Pops loved fresh fish, and how much he had loved it too.

'Give me a sec, Pops,' he said, walking up to the boys. 'About how much dollars' worth ah fish me can buy from you boys?' he asked them.

Their eyes lit up and their smiles reached their ears. 'You can give we two dollars,' they said.

'Two dollars? Me will give you two dollars each.' They couldn't believe their ears and looked at him as if he was mad. 'Me no hear nobody seh is ah deal yet,' he said.

'A deal!' they all shouted at once.

Tee gave them their money and they laughed at their good fortune. When he got back to his father, Pops asked what he was going to do with all the fish.

'What you and Mama and the boys can't eat me will eat, me love fry fish, you see, man.' That night, dinner was fish soup and fried fish with yam, callaloo and breadfruit.

As the days passed, Tee walked all over the neighbourhood. With his mother he visited the spot where Gamper and Carl had killed the large hog and where he had killed the little piglet. 'Son,' Mama said, 'all dis ah fe you, so if you ever come back ah yard fe live, you can bil you house pon dis land.'

Tee smiled. Then they saw a girl of about eighteen years coming towards them, carrying a bucket of water on her head. She greeted his mother while he stared at her, for she was tall and beautiful.

'Hey gal child,' his mother said.

'Me ah hear you Mrs Kay.'

'Mrs Dee up ah de yard deh?'

'Me tink so Mrs Kay.'

'Tell her seh me ah come look fe her.'

A little while later, Mama and Tee followed the girl to Mrs Dee's. He could remember Mrs Dee, who had been quite old when he was a boy, but she did not recognise him.

'Dis ah me washbelly bwoy, Pupatee,' Mama said.

Mrs Dee held and kissed Tee, but all he could think about was the girl with the bucket who he had seen around the back of the house. 'Mrs Dee,' he said. 'Me no too rich you know. But see thirty dollar here, fe buy you bread and milo.' She almost cried with pleasure, but he cut short her thanks by asking if he could get some water.

'Rose,' Mrs Dee called.

'Me ah come, Granny.'

'Mrs Kay son ah come fe ah drink ah water, God bless him.'

166

Tee left Mama and Mrs Dee faster than a long dog and went round to the back where Rose's and his eyes made four. She gave him the glass of water and he took a sip and then put the glass on the side and started chatting her up. 'Boy,' he told her, 'me come from England five days now an you ah de first ting me see so sweet.'

'You too lie.' She smiled.

'Ah true man, me ah come take you out one of them days. Where you want us to go, down a river go swim?'

'Ah joke, you ah joke,' she said shyly. 'Ah who dem call you?'

'Pupatee.'

'Bwoy, you relly favour you bredda Gamper weh dead, an me see no different in ah you face from you other bredda Carl. Me tink you was him, but you bigger and taller.'

'Me no even see him yet.'

'Me see him, all ah de time. Ah drive him taxi.'

'Come, we go, Tee,' Mama called. 'We go now.'

Tee took Rose in his arms and held her, saying, 'Me ah bring you ah England go marry you, you know. You would ah like dat sweety Rose?'

She smiled and blushed, and he kissed her on the cheek.

'Pupatee!' his mother called again.

'Bye, Rose,' he said. He began to turn away, but then he stopped and fished out $15 and gave it to her. Then he joined Mama and they made their way back home.

'You like de little young gal?' Mama teased.

'She's nice.'

'Well, no badda go wid you fast self an breed her up, den go back ah England, fe go mek people chat we name when you gone.'

'No, Mama.'

167

She looked at him and said, laughing, 'You stay deh bout you no man.'

Sure enough, two days later he found himself at Mrs Dee's again. Rose was there and the first thing she said to him was, 'It looks like you never know dat me did miss you,' and gave him a sweet smile. That night he stayed for supper, and the night. When he got home the next day, all Mama said was, 'You and dat young gal!'

The time passed quickly and before he knew it the weekend had come around again. On the Saturday he went with his father to the British market. Although there were plenty of shops selling West Indian food in Brixton, Tee had forgotten what a real Jamaican market was like. You could buy anything there. The place was alive with gossip, haggling and raucous laughter. Everywhere you looked there were bright colours, and the air smelt of spices and ripe fruit. There were huge piles of green bananas lying about, strings of orangey yellow ackee hanging up, sacks of spices, baskets of fish, coconuts, sugar-cane, bright yellow corn, callaloo, cho-cho, mangoes, pineapples, soursops, saltfish, live chickens, all kinds of meat and offal. There was a stall selling mouth-watering barbecued jerk, and another selling iced skyjuice. The stall-holders, most of them plump women, grinned or called out to Tee as he strolled by.

After wandering around, Tee joined Pops in the bar, where he and eight or so friends were drinking white rum and water.

'Wha happen, Pops, you all right?' he asked.

'Yeah, man.'

Everybody stopped what they were doing and had a good stare at him. Tee told the barman to make two large bottles of rum available for everyone to drink. 'Nice one, youth man, you know wha we like,' they all said.

'Ah me last son, you know,' his father said.

'So weh him did deh?' someone asked.

'Him did go ah England when him was ah little boy.'

'And now you lost one son and gain another one, you lucky, no, rass?'

Pops smiled. An old woman piped up, 'Ah wait, ah you last seed dis Putto?

'Yes, mum,' Pops said.

The lady turned to Tee and placed her hand on his chest, saying, 'Sonny, Mrs Kay always produce a child for your father if not every year, every other year, but long time ago in this very bar they all joke that him gone soft in his old age because nearly three years passed still Mrs Kay never had no big belly and they told him you back get weak now Putto, you seed bag dry up. And sonny,' she continued, 'you father bet everyone a bottle of white rum each that his back no gone weak yet and him seed bags no dry up yet. And sonny, everyone bet him he couldn't make Mrs Kay produce another youth, and the end of that year Mrs Kay had you. And me was in this very bar when you father came in one Saturday and collected his bet from everybody.'

By now everyone was laughing, and Tee joined in, but after only three shots of rum he was feeling drunk, so he stepped outside to get some fresh air. Sitting outside, he discreetly made a small joint, and was soon feeling better. When he returned to the bar, he saw that his father was unsteady on his feet so he held him up and told the barman to wrap up a bottle of white rum and a bottle of brandy, and give another bottle of rum for the house, and then he led his father away to the mules. Pops was drunk, but still able to laugh and joke all the way home.

That night Tee sat on brother Gamper's grave and as

169

he thought of him he cried his eyes and heart out. Mama came out and said, 'Son, it's good to cry but no worry yourself, because if only Gamper had remembered to say Lord forgive him his sins and have mercy on his soul then you will see him again in paradise one day, as long as you remember to ask forgiveness when your time comes.' Then he gave her the brandy and rum, and she put them away for Pops for a rainy day.

Two days later, the rain did indeed come. When he was alone for a moment Tee rolled himself a spliff and took a few hard drags, still feeling it was disrespectful to smoke ganja in front of his mother and father. Then his father suddenly appeared. 'Ah, wha dat you did ah smoke ganja?' he said.

'No, er, it is English cigarettes,' said Tee.

'Den give me a draw, no?'

All Tee could do was give it to him and stay close to watch that it didn't have any bad effect. Pops took a few draws and then gave it back to Tee who carried on smoking the joint. After a while Pops said, 'Me would love ah drink, ah white rum now, you see, man.'

'Me soon come, Pops,' he said. 'Don't move.'

Tee went and asked Mama for the bottle of rum she'd put away. She gave him two glasses and a jug of water, and plucked the rum from her room. Tee sat down with Pops, and they started drinking and talking and joking for a long time. The night was dark and the noise of the crickets and frogs sang in his ears. He looked up at the sky and the stars seemed so close he felt he could almost reach up and touch them. A shooting star sped like lightning across the sky, a beautiful sight that lingered for ever in his memory.

One morning Tee went up to Spanish Town to find Carl. Everywhere he went looking for him, he seemed to have just left. Another taxi driver said he could ride along with him, as he was bound to run into Carl in the end. They drove about for a couple of hours until the taxi man suddenly tooted and waved at a car passing them in the other direction. 'Dat look like Carl,' he said, screeching to a halt. Tee jumped out. The other car stopped a little way down the road and its driver got out. He and Tee started walking towards each other and as they drew closer it felt as if he was walking into a mirror.

'Wha happen, me bredda?' he said.

'Blood claat, Pupatee!' Carl cried, looking him over. 'Den how you look like me so much.'

'Den you ah no me brother man,' he said, and they both stood there, smiling at each other, trying to digest the fact that at long last they were together again.

'Blood claat, me bredda,' Carl said again, throwing his arms around Tee and embracing him. When they pulled apart, Carl said excitedly, 'Pupatee, me have a girl. Come, she have a twin sister, pretty, no rass, me know she ah go love you. Come, man.'

They drove in Carl's car. The streets in Spanish Town, with all their houses and flats, were very modern, but there were still trees everywhere. Eventually they reached a beautiful block of flats. Carl drove through a pair of big metal gates and parked the car. They walked up to the door of a flat and Carl pressed the bell, and then hid around the corner, telling him to stay put. Suddenly the door opened and a big, beautiful woman stood there. 'Hi, darling,' she said, wrapping her arms around his neck, kissing him and putting her tongue in his mouth. He was loving it all, but then Carl slipped out from around the corner and said, 'Yes, me catch you!'

The woman jumped back in surprise and embarrassment, but Carl burst out laughing and soon the woman and Tee joined in. 'Pupatee,' said Carl as they walked into the flat, 'dis ah me galfriend, Betsy, and dis' – he turned his head as another woman stood up – 'is her twin sister Ruth.'

Ruth smiled at Tee, showing her white teeth.

'I did ah drive down the road when Pupatee link me up,' Carl said to the women. 'Him just reach from England. Me have to do some more pick-up, is it all right if him stay here with you until me finish work?'

'Of course man, you no have to ask dat, darling.'

'Is dat all right?' Carl said to Tee.

'All right, but if is money you worrying about you need not cause me have money fe you as well as fe meself, no seet?'

'We will deal with dat later, man, but me have to pick up some people, you know.'

When Carl was gone, Tee realised that he was tired and dusty from driving around looking for him, so Betsy suggested he have a shower and a rest and it was not long before he was lying down, all fresh and clean, on a big double bed. He felt very peaceful.

When Tee had rested, he went back into the living-room and sat down with Ruth and Betsy.

'Ah bet you seh dem have some nice woman over deh,' Ruth said.

'Yeah,' he said, 'they are nice.'

'How about you, you have a nice woman in England?'

'No,' he said.

'You too untrue.'

Betsy left the room and Ruth watched him keenly. Ruth and Tee continued talking about England.

Eventually, Tee said, 'Me just come over from England and me don't know a single woman or girl. Me tink me and you could get like galfriend and bwoy-friend while me here?'

She smiled at him and her bright eyes looked right into his. Then she said, 'Me don't tink so, you know.'

Tee felt as if he had just jumped out of a plane without a parachute. Usually he had no problem with women. He tried to speak, but he couldn't get a word out. Ruth stared at him for a moment and then went to join her sister in the other room.

When Carl came home Tee told him what had happened.

'You tell her seh you love her already?' Carl asked.

'Yeah, but she seh she not too sure.'

'No worry yourself, man, no gal pickney can't get way from de breed ah Baccass family.'

They laughed at this.

'Wha you want fe do?' Carl said. 'You want fe go for a drive de four ah we and stop at one wine bar and eat and drink someting?'

'Dat sound good man,' Tee replied. 'My treat.'

'So you have no money?'

Tee still had £1,500 in notes and traveller's cheques and $800. He gave Carl £400 and another $400 and Carl smiled and put it in his pocket and went to tell the girls. They dressed up in their best and then they all drove down to the wine bar and had a few drinks and something to eat. They talked and laughed, and the more Tee watched Ruth the happier he became. Although she had been introduced to him as Ruth, Betsy and Carl called her Doll, and he began to call her Doll too. By the time they pulled up back at the flats he needed Doll more than words could tell. Doll and Betsy got out of the car and Tee climbed out too. But when Betsy saw Tee, she said, 'Weh you ah go, Pupatee?' Tee's heart felt heavy, but he covered his disappointment by stretching out his arms and saying, 'Oh, just taking some fresh air.'

They all said good-night and then the brothers drove

back to Carl's flat, where he brought out a large bottle of rum and they carried on drinking until they were overcome by tiredness.

Tee spent a few more days in Spanish Town, without any greater success with Doll, and then Carl drove him back to see Mama and Pops. Tee went for walks and hung around the house, keeping his parents company and helping out with whatever they were doing. He saw Rose once, but now his thoughts were all for Doll and he started making up a song for her.

One day he went fishing with his nephew, Ervin, and while they were by the river Ervin asked, 'So wha you ah go do with you life when you go back to England, man?'

Just at that moment he was turning over the words and tune to the song about Doll in his mind, so he said, 'I'm going to be a singer.'

'You can sing?'

'Well . . .'

'Sing one song, let me hear.'

Tee wasn't too sure, but Ervin pressed him, so he started singing his song to Doll.

Well listen, baby Doll
Girl, I've got something to tell you
I love you, yes I do
Yes, you've stolen my heart . . .

'It sound wicked man,' Ervin said when he had finished.

'You want to see de girl de song is about,' Tee told him. 'Ah she look wicked.'

The next day, Ervin came over to the house again and to his horror told Mama that Tee was going to become a singer.

174

'Him can sing good, you see, Granny.'

'You can sing, Pupatee?' Mama asked, fixing him with a doubtful look.

'A bit.'

'Well, if you want to be a singer go sing then, son. Look pon Milly, she sang one song, 'My Boy Lollypop', and son, it mashed up de whole wide world.'

The next day Carl arrived to collect Tee. Tee was surprised that the week had passed so quickly and delighted that he was returning to Spanish Town, where he could see Doll again. On the way they stopped off in Chapelton to see Joseph and Jeanie, and then hit the road to Spanish Town. A part of Tee still wanted to talk more about Gamper, his dead brother, but every time he mentioned him, people said, 'Let him rest in peace.'

When they got to Spanish Town they went straight over to see Betsy and Doll, who was wearing a dress that made her look more dazzling than ever. The others talked and joked, but Tee just sat and stared at Doll, distraught because he loved her and she did not love him. Eventually, they all started to feel hungry so Carl said they should go and eat.

'Where shall we go?'

'Me love fish,' Doll said.

'Me too,' Tee agreed.

'Nobody like fish like me,' Carl added, and to prove the point began telling a story about a time when they had gone diving for fish in a bamboo river. 'Me seh me dive to de bottom of this river's deepest hole and me was pushing my hand in holes in de root of de bamboo, feeling if any fish or crayfish or sand fish were sleeping soundly and catch dem by surprise, when me slipped my hand in dis tiny hole and inside me caught a fish. But de fish and my hand couldn't come back out same

175

time and me tried and tried, not wanting to let go of de fish, and don't forget me at de bottom of de river underwater, you know, and me run out of breath long time. So in de end, me let go of de fish, but even den my hand is stuck and me start to panic, and me give one hard pull and cut up de whole ah me hand, nearly leave me hand and fingers behind in dat hole!'

They went out and ate a delicious fish meal, but when supper was over, it was the same story with Tee and Doll. She went to bed in her flat and he went back to Carl's.

The next day, though, they were back at the flat. There was no food there, so Tee said he would buy some and cook a meal. Doll had to do something, and Carl had a job to carry out, so Betsy took him over to the market and they bought piles and piles of delicious Jamaican food. When they got back, Doll had finished her tasks and was lying out in the back yard, and he stole a look at her long sexy legs and her lovely hair, and his craving for her grew even stronger.

Back in the kitchen, he cut up the chicken they had bought and cleaned it and added salt and seasoning, and cut up the steak and seasoned that too. Then he got the frying pans hot and added oil, and started browning the chicken and steak. When they were browned and half cooked, he put them in pots, and added more seasoning, as well as onions, thyme, tomatoes and water, and left them to simmer on a low fire.

'Dat smell good,' said Carl when he returned. 'Me could eat a whole cow.'

'You know, Carl,' said Tee, as he began peeling the yams and bananas and making dumplings, 'Me love Doll so much, me even make up a song about her.'

Carl screamed out in laughter but stopped when he

saw Doll entering the kitchen behind him.

'Wha him seh?' she asked.

'Him seh him love you so much that him make up a song about you.'

'Sing it.' Doll laughed. 'Let me hear, den.'

'Me have fe peel de pumpkins,' Tee said, relieved that he had the excuse of the cooking. Doll and Carl left the kitchen, still laughing, while he put the pumpkins on to boil and then started the rice. He tasted the juices of the steak and chicken, and added some hot pepper and sweet pepper and a touch more black pepper. The food really was smelling wonderful and he had time to whip up the ingredients for a Guinness punch just as Joe had taught him years before, and then he put it in the fridge to cool.

As it was getting dark, Carl said, 'When dis food is going to finish old man?'

'Yeah,' added Doll.

'Me ah dead fe hungry,' Betsy butted in.

Tee looked up and said, 'You know something, me too.'

Tee took special care making up Doll's plate, with yam and banana and a dumpling and pumpkin and rice, and steak, and a whole chicken breast with lots of juice. Then he put the plate on a tray with a glass of Guinness punch, and took it out and presented it to Doll. Carl did the same for Betsy, and then the two of them got their own plates. When they came back into the sitting-room, Betsy said, 'You can cook nice, Pupatee.'

'Yeah, it taste nice, man!' Doll added.

'All me can seh, me bredda, Tee, it good to taste you cooking.'

Eventually, when they had all eaten their fill and the plates were cleared away, and they were sharing their second large spliff, Doll turned to Tee and smiled sweetly and said, 'Pupatee, sing de song fe me now no?'

There was nothing he could do except sing:

Well he say, listen baby Doll
I've got something to tell you
Oh yeah, I love you, yes I do
Babe, you've stolen my heart
And that's why in everything
I promise to be true . . .

He put all his heart and soul into the song, and by the time he was finished, Doll was nestled right up against him.

That night, he put on his best clothes – black slacks, white string vest, a short-sleeved baggy suede jacket and all the gold jewellery he had – and admired himself in the mirror. But when Doll came into the room she stole the show. She was dressed in blue trousers and a white silk blouse, and her skin glowed under the white silk. They went out and ended up at a wine bar, drinking and watching the people dance. Then, suddenly, Doll got up and grabbed his hand and said, 'Let's go dance.' She led him on to the dance floor and they twirled around for hours.

Back at the girls' flats, Doll got out of the car and Tee followed her, pretending to stretch and saying he was wanting some fresh air. Betsy and Carl, who were still in the car, said, 'See you tomorrow,' and drove off, and Doll led Tee by the hand inside.

'You couldn't even send one letter to me say you all right. Me tink you did gone back ah England, man,' Mama scolded.

'No, Mama.' He laughed.

'You laugh, Pupatee,' she said. 'You no remember

178

when you used to be a baby and you go way for hours and me ah call you all over de place. Pupatee! Pupatee!'

His father had a friend visiting at the time and he turned to this friend and said, 'One ah de saddest day was when him go England. But him can't complain, me live fe have ah drink with him and if me live me would ah drink it one more time.' He turned to Tee. 'When you go back, son?'

'Couple ah days, Pops.' Tee felt sad. 'Me just ah go back ah England fe work some money, buy ah truck and ah van, and come tek all dem fruits go ah market weh get waste all de times.'

'If you could ah ever do dat, son, you would ah be large,' Pops replied. 'Dat would be a good ting, son, if me live me would like fe see you do dat. All these cows and bulls going to need sensible man.'

They cut grass together and took the animals down to the river and Tee truly believed that he would return from England and tell Pops to put his feet up and relax, as he so deserved, for all his years of hard work.

The day of his departure arrived. 'If me live me will see you again if you ever come back, you hear son,' Pops said. Tee was standing facing him and he put up his hand to shake his father's, but Pops came towards him. 'Den give me ah kiss no man,' he said. They embraced and when Tee turned away he saw two long tears running down Pops's cheeks. Pops walked away and got on his mule, and headed up the hill. Tee said goodbye to Mama, and she held him and kissed him and cried as well. Then Tee turned and walked away towards the waiting car.

Joseph and Jeanie and Sakasher and Carl and Doll and Betsy all came to see him off from the airport. This time he knew what was waiting for him at the other

179

end, and he looked forward to getting back to his busy life in London. Jamaica wasn't his real home any longer. But he was sad to say goodbye to his family now that he had got to know them again, and of all the women he had known and loved he would miss Doll the most. He said his farewells and made his way towards the plane, just as he had done so many years before.

8

Drape Up

It was as cold as a freezer, and for the second time in his life Tee found it hard to adjust to the English winter after the warm sunshine of Jamaica. But he was excited to be back. He spent the first few days visiting his family and his women and finding out what had been going on while he was away. First he went to Girlie and Paulette, and gave them their presents. Next he saw Princess, then Lorna, then Iley, and then Karen, whose belly was getting bigger and bigger. Finally he went to see sister Pearl and the family in Kellett Road. They were eager to hear all about Mama and Pops and everyone in Jamaica, and pleased with the small gifts Mama had sent them.

But with all these women to support, Tee would have to get back on the streets soon. He had been on holiday for a while, and the cash from the raid before Christmas was just about gone. So he looked up Blakie and Roderick, and they all went out to do some blagging. For a few weeks, they had a good run, but then they stole some coke and Blakie got picked up by the police while in possession of half a kilo. The police made out a case that he was a Mr Big coke seller, citing the house and cars he had bought with all his criminal moneys, and he was sent down for thirteen and a half years.

Tee and Roderick were sorry for their friend but kept robbing, and Roderick recruited another couple of men to join them. Tee knew these two men from way back and wasn't sure about them, but he agreed with Roderick to give it a go. One day they set out in a stolen Ford Granada, with Roderick at the wheel. He had found out about a cash-and-carry warehouse that took its money down to the bank every Friday, and they drove there and waited outside. Eventually a man came out and climbed into his car. Roderick drove after him and when he parked near the bank and got out, Roderick pulled up and Tee and the other two jumped out as well.

The two recruits went straight into the bank, but Tee walked slowly past the man and saw his briefcase and realised he wouldn't even have to pull out the borrowed .45 which he was carrying with him. He grabbed the briefcase and turned to run away from the man, but the next thing he knew was a hard blow on the back of his neck, and he fell to the ground. When he looked up, he saw the man he had robbed standing over him in a martial arts stance.

Tee still had the briefcase in his hand, and with the other he pulled out the .45 and fired three shots over the man's head. It was the first time he had ever fired a gun, and the noise was deafening. Blam! Blam! Blam! The man backed off and put his hands in the air. 'On your face,' Tee shouted, and the man dropped to the ground, pleading for Tee not to shoot. 'I've got a wife and four children,' he cried. 'Take the money but don't shoot me.'

Tee got up and began to run. But now he had to deal with three have-a-gos who had heard the shots. He lifted the gun and fired again into the air. His pursuers froze, and Tee ran off towards the car. He heard Roderick shouting 'Watch out!' as two more have-a-gos started towards him. He lifted the gun over their heads and pulled the trigger. It only clicked. He pulled again. Click. He had run out of bullets. There was nothing for it but to run straight through them and when Tee reached the car, he opened the door, threw in the bag and shouted 'Drive!'

'Blood claat!' Roderick yelled. 'Two bike bwoys behind following.'

Tee turned and saw two motorcyclists weaving through the heavy traffic after them.

'Just reverse over dem,' Tee shouted.

'No,' said Roderick. 'Go out and deal with dem.'

Leaving the money in the car with Roderick, Tee picked up the crook lock they had forced when they had stolen the car, and jumped out. As the men approached on their bikes, Tee swung the crook lock at them aiming for their collar-bones. Both took big smacks, after which they turned around and rode off as fast as they could.

Roderick and Tee met up with the two recruits at their meeting place, and divided up the money which totalled £12,000. But there was also a bank slip for £49,000 in the case, and a fight almost broke out when the recruits accused Tee of stealing the rest. They parted on uneasy terms.

Tee went home to see Girlie and Paulette, and gave Girlie some of his takings, which delighted her. She didn't like his way of life, but if he was committing crimes, she at least wanted her share of the proceeds. Then he went out again, puzzling over the missing money. His head was still hurting from the knock he had taken, but slowly it was clearing, and it began to click that if there was missing money there was only one man who could have taken it, and that was Roderick, while Tee was dealing with the two motor-cyclists.

He headed down to Brixton and confronted Roderick.

'Old man,' Roderick said, 'me left de whole ah de money in de tiefing car, you know.' He explained he had done it so he and Tee would not have to give more to the recruits. But Tee was doubtful.

'Wha we ah go fe it now?' he suggested.

'Hold on, little Drapes,' Roderick said. 'No, we can't go fe it now, up deh hot now.'

'Why you never seh so from time you left de money?' Tee asked, still suspicious.

Roderick shrugged, and Tee left him. But he didn't go home. He went straight to where they had left the Ford Granada, waiting to see if the coast was clear and then checked the car. Nothing. Not a thing. Tee was as angry as a hive of bees, and if he had found Roderick then and there he might have killed him. But it wasn't until a week later that he finally tracked him down, climbing out of a Jaguar XJS.

'If you wasn't me friend who me did love so much, Roderick, me would lick off you head stiff stone dead,' Tee growled. He told Roderick never to come around to his flat again.

Not long after, Tee saw Roderick in a BMW coupé, and later he heard he had taken a holiday in Jamaica. A few months after that, Tee ran into him again. Roderick suggested they do another job together, but Tee turned him down. The next he heard, Roderick had recruited a couple of undercover cops for a job, and had ended up with an eight-year sentence.

A few months had passed since Tee's return from

Jamaica and he was sunk into depression. He and Girlie were arguing, and he was broke. Without Blakie and Roderick, he only seemed to make enough to get from one day to the next, and this particular day he didn't have more than a couple of quid – not even enough to take Girlie out for a drink to cheer her up. Part of him wished he had stayed in Jamaica.

With the little they had, they went to a pub in Clapham, and Tee used his last couple of quid to buy them each drinks. Then he headed into the crowds in the hope of picking a pocket to pay for the rest of the evening. He dipped his hand into a handbag and came out with only a make-up case, but as he dropped it back in again the woman felt him and grabbed at his hand. He walked away, untroubled, as he hadn't taken anything.

When he got back to Girlie, still empty-handed, she needed to go to the ladies' room. He went with her and waited outside. As he stood there, the bouncer, a giant six-foot-four black man, strode over to him.

'Dis lady claim you tief her purse and dese two police want to talk to you,' he said to Tee. He shoved him towards the two coppers, saying, 'Talk to dem, man, talk to dem.'

Tee pushed the bouncer off him and told the police that he hadn't done anything. He turned out his pockets to show them, but they still wanted to arrest him for questioning.

Exasperated, Tee dropped his trousers to show he didn't have anything on him, but they still weren't satisfied and started trying to march him out.

'You are not taking me nowhere,' Tee suddenly yelled, pushing both the policemen so hard that they flew through a pair of swing doors towards the toilets, the doors flapping after them.

The bouncer now had a grip on him, and Tee reached into his pocket and came up with a present Doll had given him before he left Jamaica, a little penknife. He didn't intend to use it, but opened the blade just in case.

'Let me go,' he told the bouncer, but the man only gripped him even harder, so Tee drew the tiny blade across his face.

By now, the furore had attracted the attention of a couple of men who knew Tee, and they ran to his rescue, shouting for help at the same time. 'Police and de chucker-outer ah beat up Drape Up!'

The two policemen pushed their way in through the swing doors to meet half a dozen of Tee's friends flying through the air like Batman and Robin, and were knocked back out again.

Tee kept shouting at the bouncer to let him go, but the man was as stubborn as a mule, so Tee slashed his face again and again. For a second, nothing happened. But then blood began to flow out from the gashes and the bouncer let go of Tee, wiped his face and sat down on the floor in a daze. Tee pushed through the swing doors, where he saw a group of youths beating the policemen with sticks and bottles. He turned round, walked back out through the pub, and headed for sister Ivy's house where they had left Paulette. Girlie was not back yet, but by the time he had bathed and changed, she had returned. She started on at him, but soon hushed up when he showed her the money he had borrowed from Ivy, and they went out again to the Blue Lagoon as if nothing had happened.

A few minutes after they had arrived, the red lights came on, which was a signal meaning the police were coming. Girlie was wearing a long coat, and Tee wrapped it around both of them, and pulled Girlie to him – though the police had a long hard look at them, they eventually left.

They danced the night away, and ended up back at the flat in Surrey Docks. In the morning they went to Ivy's to collect Paulette, and while Tee waited round the corner, Ivy's son Ray came out to tell him that the Old Bill were looking for him.

Tee turned right round and headed for Brixton. He met Boy Blue, one of the godfathers of Brixton bad bwoys, dressed in a silk suit and shirt and piled down with gold. 'Hoy, Drape Up,' he said, 'me see some police ah look fe you. Dem did have picture of you, say you dangerous and wanted! Ah wha you do, man?'

'A bit of trouble down Clapham,' said Tee.

'Well, me know one little man will sell you a visa to go State go cool out fe a while, it don't make no sense playing no hero, bad bwoy.'

'Yeah, me know,' Tee said, 'but ah no big ting.'

Tee didn't want to go to any of his main girlfriends in case the police found him there, so he went instead to see Iley, his Indian girlfriend, who no one knew about. She put him up in her flat, but every time he went outside he met people who told him the police were looking for him.

'Drape Up, de police ah look fe you so hard,' a friend said when he walked into Con's one night, 'and you in here full ah informers. Go ha country, man, or something, go chill out.'

Tee went home again to Iley, and she suggested he go and stay with her parents in Birmingham. She took him there by coach, installed him at her parents' house, and then returned to London. The house was near Winson Green prison and walking past it every day Tee would shiver at how old and dirty and cold it looked. He would end up down at a black club called the Bee Hive where he could get a draw to smoke and hang out with other West Indians.

He made friends with a couple of brothers, Suzuki (named after his bike) and Sonny. They tried to keep him clear of crime but he still picked a few pockets and did a few robberies, although he made sure he didn't do anything too risky, as he didn't want to fall into the hands of the police. One time he stole a camera, and for a while he took photographs and sold them to people, but he never made more than a few quid that way.

In the beginning Tee went out most nights, but one evening when he stayed in he noticed how tired Iley's mother was when she got home from work and started to cook dinner. He told her he could cook, and offered to do it, and from then on he cooked dinner every night. The second or third time, Iley's mother took him to the drinks cabinet and said, 'Help yourself to a drink or two, Tee.'

He took her up on this, and for the next few days he was drunk by midday. The next time she looked in the drinks cabinet she let out a scream. 'Tee,' she cried, 'you must have some worries, no one who doesn't have worries drinks so much. What kind of trouble are you in?'

Tee told her as little as he could, but that night she called up Iley and got the whole story. No matter how good his cooking was, she decided Tee had outstayed his welcome. Her advice was that he should give himself up, but he wasn't going to do that, however low he got. The following day he jumped on a train back to London.

It was a good thing Tee returned when he did, because he found that Paulette was seriously ill and crying the whole time, and Girlie had all but given up on looking after her. Tee took his little girl straight to hospital, and his first few days were taken up with visiting her.

By the time Paulette was well enough to come home again, Tee had found out how many of his friends had been arrested for the events of that night. He was lucky to have escaped so far. Karen was due to have his baby any day now, but he couldn't get her on the phone and he didn't dare show up in case the police had her place staked out. But in the end it made no difference. He was picked up two days later outside Girlie's place, and remanded in custody on three charges of GBH, as well as affray and attempted theft.

When at last Tee got bail a few weeks later, the first thing he did was call Karen. Her mother answered the phone and started on at him straight away for doing a runner.

'She had the baby ten days ago, with or without any help from you. It's a boy and a black one at that,' she said. 'And don't say it's not yours, it has your nose and your lips.'

That afternoon, Tee went round to see his first son, who Karen had named Richard.

Winter was coming around again. While Tee was waiting for his trial to come up at court and trying to keep his nose clean, his second son was born, to Princess. This one Tee helped to name. He was called Rocky.

Tee was moving quietly between one woman and the next, with none of them very happy, but none of them able to kick him out for good. The bail restrictions meant he couldn't go about his normal business, so as well as being short of cash, he was getting frustrated.

One cold rainy evening he went round to Girlie's. He hadn't been there for a few days and was looking forward to an evening in, but when he arrived he found both Girlie and Paulette dressed and ready to go out.

'Where you going in that weather outside, Girlie?' he asked.

'Oh, I'm going up Peckham to take Paulette to the Bonfire Night fair. Claire and most of the other girls and children will be there.'

Tee frowned. 'It's too wet and cold out there,' he said. 'Get changed and put Paulette to bed.'

But Girlie jumped up and said she was going to the fair and nobody was stopping her. Tee grabbed hold of her, and tried to convince her not to go. Girlie pulled herself away and made to struggle out the door, and all full of emotions and anger and upset, Tee slapped her. This only made Girlie even more angry and she started to fight, and Tee slapped her again, telling her to calm down. Eventually she did, and sullenly putting Paulette to bed she curled up herself. Tee left, hating Girlie and himself and the whole world for what had happened.

In the morning, he went back to see if Girlie was all right but she was gone. He called back again the following day, but there was still no sign of her. And as the weeks passed, and then months, Girlie and Paulette seemed to have disappeared into thin air.

That winter found Tee living with Princess and Rocky in a flat near the Oval cricket ground. He had sold his Jensen when he first went to ground, before going to Birmingham, because it was known by all the police, and as he had spent all his money, he now had neither cash nor car.

One winter day, Tee was lounging on the settee in the flat and Rocky was playing on the blood-red carpet, when Princess emerged from the bath with a towel wrapped around her head to stop her wet hair from dripping everywhere, and another around her body, from her chest to her knees. Tee took a long hard look at her and Princess smiled and said, 'What?'

'Nothing, I'm just thinking how beautiful you look, that's all, Princess.'

Princess smiled and blushed. She went over to her son and picked him up.

'OK, Rock?' she murmured. 'You all right, baby?'

Rocky, who was having a ball of a time playing with everything from his toys to the bamboo beads hung up over the front door which rattled together when you entered the flat, twisted and wriggled in his mother's arms to be put down and get on with what he was doing.

'Oh, you turn big man now, you don't want Mummy to pick you up. Go on, then, wreck the whole place as you normally do.'

She put him down and the boy happily crawled away on the carpet. She smiled to herself as she watched him.

'He don't need you, babes, but I need you,' Tee said. 'You come to me, no? You would ah never get away from me tonight, de way you look so sweet right now.'

Princess laughed. 'No, go away, all you think about is sex, food and sleep. And you do nothing but fart in your sleep. Eeyuk!' Then she grew more serious. 'You really going to fart today, tomorrow and the day after and the whole of Christmas? Because we are broke and there is no food in the house except baby food.'

'So what you want me to do?' Tee asked. 'Go and rob and tief people when I'm on bail for dis case, with the police breathing down my neck every time I step out of de house?'

'No, I'm not telling you to do nothing as such, I'm just telling you you really going to have something to fart about over Christmas with nothing in the house to eat.'

'All right, all right, me heard you. Me ah go rob some money little from now.'

Tee wasn't serious, as the last thing he wanted was more trouble with the police, so when he went out he borrowed some money from a friend and brought it back to Princess. The money fed them for a couple of days, but soon they were broke again. The best they managed for Christmas was some tinned food, chips, soft drinks and a couple of beers.

Christmas passed, and then the New Year, and with the bail conditions and the cold outside, Tee barely left the flat. But eventually it grew too much. Rocky was hungry and Tee felt desperate. He went out and walked along the cold and wintry streets to the Oval tube station and, marching in past the ticket collector, he got the train to Brixton. He walked out past the ticket collector there too. He was utterly skint, without even fifty pence in his pocket.

He made his way down the Front Line to a West Indian café where many of his friends hung out. He watched as young and old men were served with big platefuls of food, and though Tee preferred home cooking to eating out, his mouth watered at the sight and smells of all the delicious West Indian dishes. Perhaps if he had asked someone might have bought him a meal, but he was too proud. He was a robber and thief and jack of all trades. He was still a big timer in Brixton.

While he was sitting there, a man came in looking for some weed to buy. Tee saw the opportunity to take the man's money and make a commission of five or ten pounds. Not much, but better than nothing.

'How much weed you want, star?' he asked.

But just at this moment someone Tee knew entered the café, a big man named Rudy.

'Drape Up, you see Crazy Mule?' he asked.

'No, him no deh bout right now Rudy,' Tee replied,

turning back to continue his efforts to make a weed deal.

'Hey, Drape, come up here,' Rudy said.

Tee tried to ignore him, but Rudy was insistent, so he told his customer to wait.

'Wha happen?' Tee said coldly.

'Look,' Rudy replied, 'me have ah man who have eighty weights of good wicked black ash. Come, we go take it away.'

Tee hesitated. He didn't want to get involved in anything big. He should go back to his small deal. But then he thought of Princess and Rocky at home, of the bare cupboards. And anyway, stealing from drug dealers was hardly likely to bring the police down on him.

'Wha,' Tee said quickly. 'Me ready like Uncle Freddy. Come, we ah go, man.'

He left his customer behind and followed Rudy out to a blue Jaguar XJ6. A man Tee knew as Shortie was at the wheel, and also inside was none other than the great Freeman, once the biggest weed man in the whole of Brixton.

'Wha happen, Drape Up?' Freeman laughed. 'You ah de right man fe dis job, man.'

'Yo, Drape Up,' Rudy added, 'ah Mule was to come on dis job but as we can't find him we bring you. One Indian man have eighty weight ah wicked strong black ash seen at him place.'

'What kind ah place?' Tee asked.

'A hotel.'

By the time they had talked over their plans, they were pulling up at the very hotel itself in the West End. It was broad daylight, and Tee only hoped there were no police staking it out for the drugs.

Rudy carried the attaché case in which the money was supposed to be. In the lobby they were met by an

Indian man. He took them upstairs to his room, where they were confronted by the biggest, meanest black man Tee had ever seen. He made Tee feel like a midget. 'Bombo claat!' Tee thought. 'How we going to get past dat King Kong of a man?'

The Indian turned to Rudy and said, 'If you are ready to do business we will count up the money and take it from there.'

'But we don't do business like that, man,' Rudy replied. 'We have de money here in the case but we don't see no ash. Get de ash, man, and we sit down and count out money and buy ash as we go along. Not de way you want to just count my money with you larger-than-life-size bodyguard.'

'Oh no, I can't deal with you,' the Indian said. He whispered something to the black man, threw his hands in the air and walked out of the room. Shortie followed, then Rudy, and finally, reluctantly, Freeman, leaving Tee and the big man eyeing each other.

The big man looked pitifully at Tee and then asked, 'You really want to buy this hash?'

Without thinking, Tee said, 'Yeah, man. Of course man, we have de money fe buy.'

At this the bodyguard stormed out of the room, saying, 'I'm going to get it,' just as the others returned without the Indian, apparently having failed to persuade him.

'Drape Up, why you tell de man to go get de ash, you no see we can't do nothing,' Freeman said, shaking his head.

They all pushed past Tee and headed out the door, leaving him standing there, not sure what to think. Eventually, he snapped out of it and turned to follow them. Me did try me best, he thought to himself, disappointed, because he was still utterly broke. What would he tell Princess?

He followed the others out to the street and as he walked down the steps to the pavement he saw a green van park up on the road. Driving it was the bodyguard, who climbed out struggling with a bag as big as a sack of potatoes. Tee stopped and stood there, as if the deal had been done and all he was doing was waiting to take the stuff he had paid for.

'We gave de Indian man de money,' he said.

The big man nodded and carefully transferred the bag to Tee's back. Tee now walked down the steps towards the XJ6, while the three men in the car sat there goggling at him. 'Run no, Drapes,' Freeman mouthed at him, but Tee kept walking calmly. Shortie jumped out and opened the boot. Tee put the bag in, jumped in the car and they drove off, just as the Indian and the big black man appeared together on the step. Their faces were a picture, and there were whoops of joy and laughter inside the speeding car.

The gang drove straight to the Stockwell Park estate where they hid out in the house of Freeman's woman, drinking a bottle of champagne to celebrate. While the hash was being shared out, Rudy took a ball of it and began making a joint. As Tee started doing the same, Rudy looked up and said, 'Wha you ah do, Tee?'

'Me ah mek ah spliff like you.'

'All right, you goon man,' Rudy said and laughed a sorrowful laugh. 'You tink dis ash is like any ash you ever smoke, no!'

Tee carried on sipping his champagne, and eventually he had his joint rolled and lit. The first pull it was as if nothing had happened. The second he felt. The third had him wrecked out of his head in moments. Needing some fresh air, he took his share and got up. 'Me gone,' he announced and headed for the door.

'But him know him way through the estate, no?' Freeman's lady asked.

'You stay deh.' Freeman laughed. 'Drape Up know these flats and estate better than alla we in here.'

With that Tee took a big step out feeling good about Freeman's final words of respect, and went down the stairs. He climbed over a railing and walked down to another fence telling himself he was taking a short cut, and within no time he was utterly lost. But he kept climbing fences and eventually he found himself out on the road that led up to Brixton police station. He walked fearlessly past and kept going through the market until he got to a café owned by a Greek family he knew. He took his friend Memmet into the toilet, showed him a ball of the hash and said, 'Bargain, give me fifty quid.' Memmet fished out the fifty and left, smiling to himself at the thought of the profit he would make on the street selling it in fiver and tenner deals.

Tee walked on along the Front Line, telling anyone who asked that the bag he was carrying was full of Irish potatoes he had bought from the market for his queen Princess. At every opportunity he did another small deal and eventually he caught a taxi and went home to Princess and Rocky.

'Happy New Year!' he screamed when he was safely inside, taking a pile of notes and throwing it over Princess's head, then watching as they fluttered slowly to the floor.

'What have you been up to Tee?' she said, laughing with a mixture of happiness and sadness.

'No worry, babe, we safe,' he replied. 'So pick up dat money and go shopping. Buy down every shop you desire. But before you do anyting, cook me up dese tings me picked up in de market deh.'

By the end of the next day, Tee had well over a

thousand pounds and all his friends were high and dry and bigging him up, for everyone had had a treat. They soon realised the stuff was the living murder. 'Blood claat, it look like Drape Up come fe kill we off with dis ya black ash,' they all said. Tee caught a taxi home, feeling happy and mellow, but when he entered the flat he found Princess laid out on the carpet fast asleep, with Rocky also sleeping by her side.

'Princess baby, what's up?' he cried, in a panic. But Princess stirred and put a dazed hand to her head and said, 'I'm glad you came, that ash is half strong. I made a little spliff and I never even smoke it all. Look. See it in the ashtray. It almost took off my head.' That gave him a good laugh.

The following day, Tee sold even more of the hash, and when his pockets were full of money, he went off to look for a little car to buy. He came across a Fiat 124 in good order, bought it on the spot and drove it home to pick up Princess and Rocky. While they were out driving, he stopped off at Karen's house, leaving Princess sitting in the car, and gave her some money. His first son Richard was doing well, and Tee was happy he could treat them at last. Then they were off again. Life was good once more, and the bad times seemed long gone.

And so life continued for Tee from day to day – good days, bad days, growing older. Slowly the months passed and the date of the trial arrived. For several days Tee went to court and listened to the evidence against him. Eventually the lawyers had finished their cases, and the judge had summed up and it was left only for the jury to make their decision. It was the end of the day, so the judge told the court to reconvene in the morning.

That night Tee drove sorrowfully around his old haunts and then, more in hope than expectation, cruised past the old flat in Surrey Docks where he and Girlie had moved in together some four years earlier, so full of life and dreams. He had been by so many times without seeing any sign of life that when he looked up and saw the twinkle of a light in the window he could not believe his eyes. He blinked and looked again. The light was still there. He slammed his foot on the brakes, and ran up the stair. He was so excited he bent down and looked through the letter-box. There indeed were Girlie and Paulette.

'Girlie,' he called, for he did not have his key.

'Mummy, it's Daddy,' Paulette cried.

Girlie opened the door and looked sadly out at him, though Paulette rushed to him and hugged his legs. Tee reached out and pulled Girlie towards him and held her in his arms. He wanted to tell her in a million ways how sorry he was and how much he loved her and the kid. But all he could manage was, 'I love you, Girlie.'

'Do you?'

'I'm sorry I slapped you, babes, I was wrong to hit you.'

She pulled herself free and stood there looking at him, and he could sense that she was slowly coming round.

'Oh, give me a kiss, Girlie,' he said.

'Do you really want me to?'

'Of course, babes, you don't know how I miss you and love you and need you. I've been worried over you. Where have you been?'

'At my friend's house in East London.'

And eventually she gave him his kiss.

It was now well past Paulette's bedtime so Tee put

her to bed and tucked her up. Then he returned and took Girlie to bed too, and they lay in each other's arms, talking about the past and the future. They promised they would start again and make a go of things, though of course they both knew what the next day's judgement might mean. Then they made love and went to sleep.

In the morning, Tee got up and dressed and kissed Girlie goodbye and drove down to the court, to face the jury's verdict and see what life would bring.

All Fourth Estate books are available at your local bookshop or newsagent, or can be ordered direct from the publisher.

Indicate the number of copies required and quote the author and title.

Send cheque/eurocheque/postal order (Sterling only), made payable to Book Service by Post, to:

Fourth Estate Books
Book Service By Post
PO Box 29, Douglas
I-O-M, IM99 1BQ.

Or phone: 01624 675137

Or fax: 01624 670923

Or e-mail: bookshop@enterprise.net

Alternatively pay by Access, Visa or Mastercard

Card number:

Expiry date   ....

Signature   ....

Post and packing is free in the UK. Overseas customers please allow £1.00 per book for post and packing.

Name   ....

Address   ....

                    ....

                    ....

Please allow 28 days for delivery. Please tick the box if you do not wish to receive any additional information. ☐

Prices and availability subject to change without notice.